Olive

The Other Reindeer

A CHRISTMAS ADVENTURE

Olive

The Other Reindeer

A CHRISTMAS ADVENTURE

Bruce Kilby

Illustrations Christine Lee

Fireside Stories Publishing

Published by Fireside Stories Publishing

#8, 5662-208th Street,
Langley, B.C., Canada
V3A 8G1

Editing, Interior Design, and Cover Design
Wendy Dewar Hughes, Summer Bay Press

Cover Art and Chapter Illustrations by Christine Lee

E-book readers may obtain the accompanying chapter plates for youngsters to colour can be downloaded from the website at Firesidestoriespublishing.com.

Print ISBN: 978-0-9920742-6-5
Digital ISBN: 978-0-9920742-7-2

To all those who have lost furry best friends and still miss them.

ARCTIC REGION

CHAPTER ONE

Home

Santa Claus and his reindeer team were wasting no time. Flying at top speed, they made their way back home to the North Pole after their last stops in American Samoa and Hawaii. They were all exhausted. They had delivered so many gifts, toys, and curiosities for all the good girls and boys around the world, all in one night.

Santa giggled with excitement at the warm thought of getting home to his wife, Carol—Grandmama to those close to her and Mrs. Claus to the rest of the world—and to his elves and all the other reindeer. Christmastime was his favorite time of the year and now that his job was complete, it was his turn to unwind after another busy season. Following his tiring journey, there was nothing he liked better than having a relaxing Christmas morning with Mrs. Claus and all his helpers he affectionately called, "The Elves". He knew they would sing Christmas carols, share stories and gifts, enjoy each other's company, and lovingly remember what the meaning of Christmas was all about.

His mouth watered at the thought of the aromas, those wonderful smells that filled the air only at Christmastime: cinnamon, peppermint, mandarin oranges, and always the

Christmas dinner followed by a hearty portion of Christmas pudding. Santa *loved* his Christmas pudding.

As the sleigh flew through the night, he imagined gulping down his favorite Christmas breakfast of two poached eggs and bacon, and a stack of syrup-drizzled pancakes topped with whipped cream and fresh blueberries. Mrs. Claus tried very hard to have her Nicholas eat lighter meals, though she knew it was an almost impossible task. More than once she'd had to let out the seams in his vest and his trousers, or punch another hole in his ever-tightening belt.

Santa knew she would declare, as she did every year: "You mustn't eat so fast. It's very bad for your digestion." He realized that she also knew he had eaten a lot of sugary treats left by well-wishing children on his long voyage around the world. But she was never sure of precisely how many he'd eaten. On this trip alone Santa had lost count after the four thousand, two hundred, and twenty-seven cups of hot chocolate, and the twelve thousand, six hundred, and forty-two glasses of milk and eggnog he had drunk. He had munched countless numbers of cookies that had been left out for him by kind and thoughtful children around the world.

Even the reindeer couldn't count the many carrots and slices of apple that had been left for them, but they enjoyed every tasty crunch of them. Santa knew that even though Mrs. Claus served healthy meals with plenty of vegetable throughout the year, he could count on her offering him a steaming cup of hot chocolate stacked with marshmallows to accompany his favourite breakfast. He loved his hot chocolate and she couldn't deny him this treat after he had worked so hard on such a long journey.

The tuckered out reindeer crew took the same route home as they had done for as long as they could all remember. They knew it by heart and could probably fly it blindfolded. As their tired legs trudged on in a rhythmic glide in time with the soft jingle bells on their harnesses, each reindeer had warm thoughts of his own family and couldn't wait to get home and nuzzle tenderly with each loved one.

Rudolf was thinking of his wife, Clarice, and their son Rollo; Dasher thought of Springer, and Prancer longed to see his daughter Olive who, as everyone knew, had had a tough time adjusting to Rudolph when he came on scene. She used to laugh and call him names, and play tricks on him during reindeer games. That is, until Rudolph became a hero to all after saving Christmas for Santa on one foggy eve.

Almost on autopilot they headed northward over the string of Alaskan islands known as the Aleutians. No matter how much Santa tried to encourage them, the reindeer were no longer interested in playing their favorite in-flight pastime of Carrot Catch. They had simply eaten far too many carrots and apples already. They were just plain too tired and too full. Now they just wanted to get home.

"Come, my beauties, one more game," Santa urged, trying to keep their spirits up while tossing another carrot stick for Dasher to catch.

"I couldn't eat one more bite, Papa Nick," Dasher replied as the carrot fell and disappeared into the clouds below. "But thank-you."

"Ho, ho, ho! How about a sing-a-long then? *Jingle Bells* perhaps?"

A groan rose up from the nine reindeer. How many times can we sing *Jingle Bells, Santa's Coming to Town,* or *Here Comes Santa Claus*? Their legs were so fatigued it was all they could do to pull the sleigh.

"Okay, okay, my beauties," Santa chuckled. "I know we are all exhausted but we'll all be home soon and you can all get a well-deserved rest on a fresh bed of straw that I know the elves have prepared for you."

Each reindeer eagerly nodded his head. The bells on their harnesses rang a little louder, the familiar jingles spurring them on with a new burst of energy.

Santa was pleased and relieved that all those countless gifts the children had anxiously wished and waited for all year long had finally been carefully placed under each Christmas tree, in the stockings carefully hung on the fireplace, or laid at the foot of a bed. He recalled each name, checked his list for the special toy a child had wished for in letters sent to him or the whispered reminder in his ear when they excitedly visited his Helpers in the shopping malls and on the streets. Every Santa's Helper had passed on each child's wish. Once he had carefully placed the gift and had seen a child sleeping, he quietly said his or her name, blessed each one, and wished each one a happy and merry Christmas.

He was thrilled that no prying eyes of a small child or a curious adult, wanting to find out if he really did exist, had discovered him while he placed his colourfully and neatly-wrapped gifts. To Nicholas, the mystery of Santa Claus—or Father Christmas in some places—was what kept the excitement, the wonder, and the mystique of Christmas alive for all these years.

There were, as in every year, a couple of close calls. In Norway, he was forced to rapidly shrink and hide behind a stuffed teddy bear that he had just placed beside a decorated tree when a small child, sleepily rubbing her eyes, came down the stairs to see what all the noise was about.

"Is that you, Santa?" she asked drowsily. Seeing nothing, she wandered back to bed before her mother heard her.

Another time, in Canada, he signalled his reindeer to stomp their hooves just in time to send three little children scampering back upstairs to confirm their suspicions of Santa's arrival. Then he put his finger to his nose and in a twinkle, raced back up the chimney, jumped in his sleigh with a hearty, "Ho, ho, ho!" took off in a blur to the next house.

He knew the children would be watching for him from their bedroom window so he turned, waved his white-gloved hand and winked. He saw them scurry off, screaming with delight to tell their unbelieving and very sleepy parents that the jolly elf had once again visited them. Santa so loved this "hide and seek" game and found it as exciting as the children did.

Santa took great pleasure and delight in filling a stocking with goodies and leaving a nice toy or playful gift under the Christmas tree for all the little children. He looked for each child's good deeds that they had done throughout the year. Had they been kind to each other, listened to their parents and their teachers, were they nice to their friends, cousins' brothers and sisters? He was always saddened and a little disappointed when some children just couldn't be good for a whole year. This year however, was better than most. Santa was pleased that it had been an excellent year for especially good children.

This year however, was better than most. Santa was pleased that it had been a successful year for good children because when he looked in the back of the sleigh, a burlap sack of coal was still nearly full and only two gifts remained undelivered. One had been for a little boy who had moved this very night without leaving a note of where he was going and the other had been undelivered because a little girl had forgotten her promise to be good on the very eve of Santa's arrival. She was spiteful and mean to her sister, refused to do her chores, and wouldn't help her brother wrap the carefully handmade necklace he was planning to give their mother.

Three strikes all in one night! he thought, frowning. *That will never do. That will never do indeed!* He had reluctantly left a large piece of black coal in her stocking. Perhaps she will be better behaved next year, he hoped.

On this Christmas Eve, the jolly group had had more than their fair share of bad weather. Heavy winds, rain, sleet, and snow met them all along the way. England was unusually rainy, even for England! Santa had cinched the toy bag tightly to make sure the toys didn't get soaked. In Russia they had met with a terrible ice storm across the entire country, and blinding snow and whiteout conditions across the Canadian prairies had a driving them off path several times. Rudolph's nose barely lit the way through such dreadful conditions but they forged on, got back on course, and made all the stops.

The reindeer had worked harder than usual and were now weary. They flew as though their legs had lead weights tied to them rather than bells. It was no wonder that Saint Nicholas and his band of nine famous reindeer grew drowsy now that they were on the final stretch toward the arctic and home. After all, the mythic crew had been up for over twenty-four hours delivering thousands upon thousands of toys.

Now Santa's mind began to wander and his head nodded. Dasher glanced over his shoulder and saw his best friend's eyes droop. It wouldn't take long before Santa was dreaming once again. The reindeer snickered. No matter what weather they had been through, Santa had once again fallen asleep just as he had done every year since he began leading the team so long ago.

"What do you think Papa Nicholas is dreaming about?" Dasher asked Vixen.

"I think Santa is dreaming of those pancakes and syrup, sugared plums, and gingerbread cookies," Vixen guessed.

"Mama Claus always makes sure the goodies are hot and ready upon our return," Prancer added.

This time Santa was actually dreaming of something else. He hoped Mrs. Claus would love the shawl he had secretly knitted for her while hidden in the mailroom behind the stacks of letters received from the children around the world. He had lovingly wrapped it in bright red paper with a lovely green bow and placed it under the tree, being sure to hide it amongst all the gifts selected for each elf.

Santa smiled in his sleep and dreamed on.

CHAPTER TWO
Something Strange

The bitterly cold, late December wind blew fiercely as the little band trudged on through the darkness toward the tundra. Once more it began to snow heavily and before long the sleigh was engulfed in an all-out tempest. Compared to the weather of previous years, this storm swirled around them angrier, darker, and more violent, as if the blizzard had a life of its own and resisted every move made by the intruders.

The valiant reindeer sensed danger. "This is no regular storm," Vixen shouted above the wind's fury as a tremor of wariness rippled through her.

"We've gone through these before," Comet replied, his shoulders sagging.

"Not like this," Cupid bleated, eyes wide. "I feel it in my antlers. This is unmistakably different."

"Oh, you and your antlers!" Donner scoffed. "You always feel something or other in your antlers."

"But I do! I have extra-sensory antlers!" Cupid protested.

"Sure you do," Donner replied with a smirk.

"Relax everyone, don't get so excited. We're nearly home," Dasher's deep, soothing voice settled the reindeer once again into the rhythmic motion of running on air. Meanwhile Santa, fast asleep, unconsciously swatted at snowflakes that tickled his nose.

In the lead, Rudolf dipped his head to protect his eyes from the stinging ice crystals that formed on his eyelashes as they flew through the dense grey clouds. The blizzard howling down from the Arctic Circle was the worst he'd seen in the seventy years of helping guide Santa's sleigh. Straining, he could barely make out the distant lights of Bethel to the west. I*t won't be long now*, he thought. Far over to his right he knew the Katamai volcanoes reached up high, but not as high as their next climb around Mount Denali, the massif once called Mount McKinley. To avoid being seen by the young children's ever-sky-scanning eyes he knew Santa would guide them to skirt the tree line around the mountain and head north through the deep forests of Denali National Park.

Snow settled on the reindeers' backs and clung to Santa's red overcoat and cap. His red coat grew as white as his beard. The reindeers' bridles and bells no longer jingled, as they were now frozen stiff and coated in ice. Antlers became heavy with frost. Snow piled up on the empty sacks in the back of the sleigh now that most of the toys had been moved out. The reindeers' tears and their steamy breath froze as soon as the moisture hit the glacial air.

Opening his eyes for a brief second, Santa looked around. "Looks like it's going to be a long, long winter, my pets!" he called out, shaking snow off then curling up to nod back to sleep.

Rudolf knew that Dasher and Dancer, being the oldest, would be the first to become exhausted and might have a hard time keeping up with the rest of the team. But as always, they poured all the remaining strength they could muster into the final push. He also knew that they, as with all the others, had hearts of amazing courage and would boldly trudge on, no matter what, to keep the Santa's sleigh aloft and get them home safely. The annual trek to deliver toys was what they lived and trained for all year long but once they knew the last toy was delivered, all the excitement and energy seems to drain from their tired bodies.

As they trudged onward, once again the reins slipped from Santa's fur-lined gloves as he slumped farther down in his leather seat, sound asleep. A sudden blast of wind buffeted the sleigh jostling him awake. "Huh, what?" he muttered, sitting up and rubbing his eyes.

Santa looked around to check their location. Pretending, as always, that he hadn't fallen asleep in the first place, he called out, "Mush, my beauties! I know you are as tired as I but it won't be long now. Soon we'll be home in our warm cozy beds. On Dasher, on Dancer, on Prancer and Vixen, on Comet, on Cupid, on Donner and Blitzen!" When the reindeer heard his familiar refrain a burst of new energy and spirit invigorated them.

With the rhythm and motion of the sleigh, it was not long before Santa once again slouched back in the sleigh's curved seat and drifted off to sleep once more. He trusted Rudolf and the rest of the reindeer to find their way home.

Onward the team flew through the bitter storm, past Manley Hot Springs and far into the north. The last marker far below them would be Prudhoe Bay and not long after, they would reach the North Pole.

Prancer's thoughts turned to his daughter Olive, hoping she was not causing any trouble in the reindeer pen. Comet thought of his son Bollo, and Cupid her daughter Snowball and longed to be cosy in their stalls full of fresh straw.

"I'm soooo full," Dasher said.

"Me too," chimed the chorus behind him.

"Maybe just one more of Mamma Claus's butter tarts when we get home," Blitzen suggested, rolling his eyes at the thought.

"I would explode if I ate another bite!" Cupid replied.

Santa always shared the treats he received because he could never refuse a child's thoughtfulness, but by the time they had gone around the world there was no way their stuffed tummies could hold another crumb!

Every year Santa faithfully promised to lose a few pounds he couldn't resist a sugar-coated cookie with coloured sprinkles. All the Reindeer knew they weren't supposed to eat cookies or hot chocolate either. Again this year, they had all agreed to only eat carrots but that promise was broken after the first stop when Santa rose from the chimney with mouth-watering gingerbread cookies to share and they couldn't resist. There was always next year…

As they flew over the dark forest, Blitzen suddenly lifted his head and sniffed. "What is that smell?"

Roused from their weariness, the others sniffed too, and smelled the strange electrical energy in the air. Then Dasher saw a bizarre blue ball of light hurtling up toward them from below.

"What is tha…?" The blue light engulfed the startled team.

"Aaaaa!" Comet cried out, terrified.

"Whoa!" shouted Santa, instantly awake, and shielding his wide eyes with a gloved hand.

"Look out!" screamed Rudolf, but it was too late.

CHAPTER THREE
Where's Santa

"Oh dear, oh dear. It's well past his time," Mrs. Claus muttered, pacing back and forth across the checked kitchen floor. She glanced at the clock again. The team was late. "My Nick and the reindeer should be home by now, safe and sound." She wrung her hands and peered out the window into the blinding snow.

Turning from the window and picking up a wooden spoon, she stirred the pot of chicken soup on the stove for the forty-ninth time. Then she put the spoon down and hurried to the south-facing window to see if the familiar sleigh with Nicholas and her beloved reindeer had appeared.

Nothing.

Nothing but howling wind and raging snow. One little glimmer of Rudolf's nose off in the distance was all she needed. It would tell her they were nearly home. But she saw no sign of the red glow.

"He should be home by now," she murmured again.

"Don't worry so, Mama Claus, they will be home soon," Alabaster said to ease Mrs. Claus's mind. "I'm sure they will. You know they always do."

"I hope you're right, Alabaster," Mrs. Claus replied meekly.

As head elf, it was Alabaster's job to read all incoming letters to Santa. As the night wore on, he had been carefully re-checking the Naughty and Nice list one final time to make sure the crew had not missed one child's name. "Papa Nick has never missed a Christmas at home," he said, running his finger down the long list.

If a child's name had been missed, it meant the delivery became much harder to carry out. He hoped he wouldn't have to try to get a missed gift to a deserving child this year. Extraordinary arrangements would have to be made to secretly get the present to the little one. A special envoy would have to deliver the gift once Santa and the reindeer were at home, an official Santa's helper, such as an uncle or aunt, or even a stranger who might want to do a good deed without being seen. Sending elves to make a delivery was a last resort. If children spotted an elf…he hated to think what a stir a captured elf might cause.

"He has only been this late once before," Mrs. Claus said. "It was the year he had to get Rudolf to lead the team in the fog?"

"I remember, Mrs. Claus. I certainly do. That was a very bad year indeed. I hope nothing has happened to them."

"He always says, 'there's nothing like being home with the family on Christmas Day.' It's his favourite day." She gazed longingly at the comfy but empty overstuffed chair by the fire. Heaving a deep sigh, she gazed around the living room that had been carefully prepared and lovingly decorated. The Christmas tree in the corner of the room smelled of fresh pine, now aglow with colourful lights, tinsel, and special ornaments. Most of the decorations were handmade and carefully placed on the tree in just the right places. Nicholas loved to pick up a special ornament from wherever he went, but he especially loved the ones children had handmade for him and had left lovingly beside a few cookies or a glass of milk.

Nestled neatly under the tree's lowest branches lay stacks of presents, piled high. For days the excitement had been mounting, especially amongst the childlike elves.

Nicholas' slippers lay by his chair next to the fire to keep them warm while the music box sweetly chimed *Silent Night* and other Christmas carol favourites. The room was cozy and warm, just perfect for Santa's return after his long, cold trip.

Christmas Day at the North Pole was like many homes in the world. After the rushing around trying to finish those last little things that make the day special, everyone gathered around the Christmas tree to enjoy the day with each other, sing Christmas Carols, and open gifts.

Every year Santa reminded the elves of the true meaning of Christmas. Rather than a mad dash of gift opening, the elves had to wait while Santa explained that Christmas was not only about the giving and receiving of presents, but about God's gift to mankind, His Son. It was the time to think of the less fortunate, those in need, and those going to bed hungry. The elves became quiet as each one promised to work harder until all children of the world would one day feel the joy of Christmas.

Then Mrs. Claus surprised her Nicholas with a gift, something small and carefully wrapped. He always chuckled and cried, "Ho, ho, ho, what do we have here?"

"Oh, Nicholas, it's nothing much but I hope you like it," Mrs. Claus replied, beaming.

He liked to pick it up, carefully shake it, put it up to his ear to see if it made a sound, and then taking his time, try to guess what it was. The whole gang shouted, "Open it, Santa; please open it!"

"Somebody put a lot of love in wrapping this fine present," he would say giving his wife a loving wink and smile. It was never about the gift but the thought that was put into it. Once open, he carefully folded the paper and put it aside, sending the elves into a frenzy of excitement. They hadn't much patience.

Mrs. Claus was amazed at the gift he gave her, wondering, "How did you know this is just what I wanted?"

Afterward they played games, enjoyed the home-baked cookies and treats Mrs. Claus had prepared, and reflected on how blessed they were. Santa sat in his comfy armchair and had his long-awaited nap before supper while the elves played with their new toys.

Wonderful smells of roast turkey, goose, or sweet ham wafted through the air. After asking the blessing, they all eagerly ate the delicious dinner Mrs. Claus had prepared until those little tummies were about to burst! And for dessert, the elves took turns guessing: Would they have Christmas pudding topped with whipped cream? Apple pie and ice cream? Perhaps trifle, or Christmas log cake? It was such a wonderful day!

Mrs. Claus sighed as she worriedly looked out the window once more. *Would they even have a Christmas this year?* she wondered.

"St. Nicholas always says to give thanks and to appreciate each other," Babbo said, wandering into the kitchen.

"He would never miss Christmas Day," little Pukki added, hugging Mrs. Claus.

"Never Christmas Day," echoed Ripplo.

From the workshop, the elves trailed in to comfort Mrs. Claus. But she could tell that they were worried, too. "Well, my dears, let's not get too down-hearted. He's only a little late." She put on a brave smile. "You know Nicholas never likes to see sad faces when he comes home."

"No, never," they agreed, nodding.

"I'm sure Rudolf and the other reindeer are pulling as fast as they can," she reminded them.

"Maybe they were just delayed by this bad storm," Alabaster suggested.

The elves' heads bobbed silently but didn't look at all sure.

"Now, have we cleaned up the workshop?" Mrs. Claus asked to change the subject. "Are the paint tins put away and the brushes properly cleaned? It was quite a mess in there after the sleigh took off."

"Yes, Mama Claus." said Pere Noel and Papai Noel together.

"Are all the electronics, computers, and scanners unplugged?"

"Yes, of course, Mama Claus" answered Sparky.

"And are the stables ready? You know how much Prancer likes his fresh oats sprinkled with a few cranberries."

"Yes, Mama Claus," said Rando. "I also put down some extra straw for Dasher and Dancer to make it extra soft."

"And all the Christmas presents are in their stalls," Sparkles confirmed.

"Very well, my dears." She looked at the assembled group and slumped into a chair. "Oh, what shall we do?" she moaned.

The forlorn elves quietly turned to look out the windows, searching for any sign of movement and straining their large ears for the jingle of bells. But only arctic shadows and driving snow answered back.

Morning turned into afternoon and afternoon turned into evening, and still there was no sign of Santa and the team. Mrs. Claus frantically paced the floor. "What to do? What to do?" she repeated, staring out each window as she passed.

"I could go out and look for them," Alabaster suggested.

"I can't let you do that. You'd freeze to death in no time at all."

"But what if he's lying out there hurt?" asked Bibbo.

"I won't hear of it." Mrs. Claus turned to Alabaster. "Not only that, as head elf, you need to be here to keep the toyshop going. Next Christmas will be upon us soon enough."

"And your pointy ears would be spotted right away," said Rando.

"And your pointy shoes," added Sparkles with a vigorous nod.

"But what if something really serious has happened?" Alabaster wailed.

"Like a crash," said Ripplo.

"Shot by hunters," said Pere Noel and Papai Noel together.

"They have always missed before," Mrs. Claus replied, wringing her hands.

"But maybe..." said Sparky

"Oh, please don't talk that way. We can't lose Santa," Alabaster demanded.

"I couldn't stomach losing my dear Nickolas, either," agreed Mrs. Claus. "We must *do* something."

"Yes, we must," said Ripplo.

"We must," echoed Pere Noel and Papai Noel.

"But what, Mama Claus?" asked Alabaster.

"Someone must go find them. Someone we trust and who would not appear suspicious to the animal or human world," Mrs. Claus began.

"Well you can't go, you're too old…" Sparky blurted, then blushed. "I, uh…"

"I beg your pardon?" Mrs. Claus wondered if she had heard correctly.

"I mean…"

"And the elves can't go, so that leaves only the young reindeer," Ripplo said, abruptly diverting Mrs. Claus' attention.

"They can't go! They are way too young," chorused Pere Noel and Papai Noel shaking their heads.

"Ripplo is right. We only have the other reindeer." Mrs. Claus gazed at the hopeful little faces gathered round about her.

"But who? They all seem so little," Alabaster said.

"And untrained," added Rando.

"It could be dangerous out there," Alabaster warned.

"At least it isn't hunting season," Bibbo murmured.

Alabaster shot him a sharp look. "There are more dangers out there than just the hunters."

"But whoever we choose must be able to go about their mission without being noticed," said Mrs. Claus.

Rando gasped. "They cannot be seen as one of Santa's reindeer or they would be captured and put in a zoo."

"That means no warm, comfy, red blankets," lamented Ripplo.

"Or jingle bells," said Pere Noel and Papai Noel, eyes wide.

Alabaster began pacing the floor, back and forth, back and forth. "So who will we send? Let me see...there's Bollo, Snowball..."

"Olive, Rollo..." Bibbo followed Alabaster's path across the kitchen tiles and back again.

"Olive?" said Pere.

"She's come a long way since her days of making fun of our Rudolf," said Rando, standing up straight and looking around at the others.

"I'm not so sure," said Mrs. Claus, anxiety creasing her brow. "She still seems a little immature."

"How about Rollo then?" chimed in Noel and Papa Noel.

"That's it! I'll ask Rollo!" Mrs. Claus said. "I'm sure Rudolf won't mind."

"He always gets lost!" Bibbo cried. "We can't send him."

Mrs. Claus shook her head. "Oh, that won't do at all."

"Olive is the most experienced on the practice runs," Alabaster told her.

"She gets lost too!" declared Bibbo.

"But she is the most experienced."

"But she's never been on her own...out there!" Rando reminded him.

"I don't think we have much choice," Mrs. Claus said finally, getting to her feet. "Let's go visit the stables."

CHAPTER FOUR
Olive's Dangerous Mission

As usual, the courtyard air was calm, fresh, and crispy cool. The enchanted dome, a magical sphere that covered and protected Santa's home and buildings, not only kept the whistling winds and severe cold out but protected Santa's home and workshops from polar bears, the prying eyes of satellites, and the never-ending aircraft that flew overhead.

In the courtyard outside the stable, Olive and Rollo were playing one of their favourite reindeer games of chase with the other young reindeer. Mrs. Claus entered the patio unnoticed to find Olive leaping, kicking up her heels, laughing with glee, and calling out the names of the other reindeer—a little too rough and tumble in Mrs. Claus' opinion.

"I thought we had learned our lesson after our incident with Rudolf, Miss Olive," Mrs. Claus said, gently interrupting the play. "I believe you promised never to laugh and call others names again."

Olive stood still and hung her head. "Yes, Grandmama Claus. I'm sorry."

"Very well then." She turned toward the other young reindeer. "Rollo, are you and the others all right?"

"Yes, Grandmama Claus, I'm okay," he replied, a little out of breath and flushed in the cheeks.

"You go see your Mama now, young man. I need to speak to Olive alone for a minute."

"Of course, Grandmama Claus," he said, bounding back to his mother.

When she was alone with Olive, Mrs. Claus lowered her voice. "I have something very important to ask of you. Come close."

Olive obediently sprang up next to her.

"I'm afraid what I have to ask you to do might be dangerous indeed," Mrs. Claus began.

"Very dangerous," Alabaster agreed gravely.

"What is the matter, Grandmama?" Olive glanced from Mrs. Claus' face to Alabaster's and back again.

"Santa has not returned yet from his sleigh ride," she said, aware of the other reindeer leaning toward her. As soon as the words left her mouth they instantly stopped whatever they were doing and stared.

"Oh my, I hadn't noticed. He is indeed very late," Olive said, looking up at the clock. "I guess I lost track while playing..."

"That's okay," Mrs. Clause interrupted, raising her arms to calm the anxious reindeer.

"We think something serious may have happened," Alabaster said, "because not only Santa is missing, but so is the entire reindeer team." A collective gasp rose from the assembled reindeer.

"Even Papa Rudolph?" Rollo squealed from across the yard.

"And Papa Prancer?" cried Olive.

"Yes, your papas and mamas are missing and we need someone to go find them," Mrs. Claus informed them all.

"I volunteer!" Rollo shouted.

Mrs. Claus smiled tenderly. "Don't be in such a rush, little one. I know you are brave and I appreciate that you are willing to go but you are young and not quite ready. And I hear your navigation skills need a little tweaking. That is why I need to talk to Olive."

"I will certainly go…" Olive said cautiously, though she too had skipped a few lessons of map reading.

"Before you agree you should know it will be very dangerous out there. You have never travelled past the dome without Santa," Alabaster told her firmly.

"I'm not scared," she said bravely. She had never been outside the dome even *with* Santa.

"You should be, Olive. Even if you get past the polar bears and arctic ice, you'll face many dangers in the forests and the human settlements," Mrs. Claus warned.

"Like bears, mountain lions, and wolves…" added Babbo.

"Don't scare her any more than necessary," Rando snapped.

"Well, she needs to know…"

"I'm still not scared," she repeated with a quaver in her voice. "I think."

The other reindeer in the yard snickered.

Mrs. Claus spun around. "Hush, all of you, unless one of you would like to volunteer to go with her." She raised one eyebrow.

The other reindeer suddenly became quiet, turning their heads to avoid Mrs. Claus's glare. Rollo stepped forward again but his mother tugged him back.

"But Mom!" he protested.

"Not on your life, young man."

"Now Olive, I appreciate your eagerness and your courage, but it will be perilous out past the protection of our enchanted dome," Mrs. Claus told her.

"I'll be okay, Grandmama," she said, though she felt far from certain.

"I wouldn't send you unless I thought you stand the best chance of finding your Papa Prancer, Rollo's Papa, Grandpapa Nick, and the rest."

"I know, Grandmama. I'm ready. Which way should I go?"

"I suggest south," said Rollo.

"Of course, I go south!" Olive retorted. "We can't go anywhere from here but south!"

"Now stop it the both of you," Mrs. Claus said with a sigh. "That bickering is what gets you both into trouble."

"Yes, Grandmama," they said in unison, glowering at each other.

Getting to the business at hand, Alabaster turned to Olive. "He would cut across the Pacific Ocean from the Samoan Islands and past Hawaii. Then he would follow the Aleutian Islands to stay close to land, across Alaska to the Beaufort Sea."

"Okay."

"He would be flying on to Banks Island in Canada," Alabaster continued, "and up the edge of Ellesmere Island, which is part of the Queen Elizabeth Islands, to the outpost of Alert."

"Uh huh," Olive replied.

"Then follow the 60° longitude line back to the North Pole," Alabaster concluded. "It's easy."

"Uh…"

Alabaster could read the confusion one Olive's face. "He would cut across the Pacific Ocean from Hawaii..." he repeated.

"I heard you, but..."

"It's simple. You just reverse the course and look for him along the way."

"But, but..." Olive stammered.

"But what?" Alabaster snapped.

"I *heard* what you said but what is a longitude?"

Alabaster slapped his palm against his forehead. "Santa has talked about it every year. You should know this."

"Maybe he said that to you elves, to Grandmama Claus, or to my Papa, but not to us younger reindeers," she protested.

"Oh." Alabaster remembered that the juvenile reindeer didn't get atlas training until they learn to fly properly. Olive was a beginner at best.

"You need to fly that-a-way," Mrs. Claus said, pointing her arm in the direction of the settlement known as Alert. "I hope you don't have to go far to find them but stay on course in the direction I'm pointing and when you see the small outpost lights of Alert, turn right and follow the coast."

Olive nodded. "I get it," she said.

"If you don't find them by then, you have to travel some way before you see the lights of Inuvik. If you haven't found them by then and turn right again."

"Okay. I think I can do that."

"Keep heading southwest. Look for the largest mountain and circle it." Alabaster explained, pulling a map from his pocket and unrolling it. His finger landed on a spot. "It's called Denali. Then if you don't see any sign of them, continue on until you run out of land."

"Then what?"

"There is no 'then what'," Mrs. Claus said.

"What do you mean, Grandmama?"

"Because if they went down in the ocean, not you nor anyone else will never find them," she said sadly. "All will be lost."

A great collective gasp and much concerned muttering came from the gathered herd, still listening to every word.

"Oh my!" Olive said, her eyes wide.

"Let's not linger on something that has not happened," Mrs. Claus said, drawing herself up. "We will find him, I'm sure of it."

The entire group looked as though the air had been sucked out of them. They all yearned for a sign of hope to dispel the dismal atmosphere.

"Really, I'm sure of it!" Mrs. Claus declared.

The elves cheered, and the reindeer snorted and stomped their hooves in support, though not completely enthusiastically. They would sooner believe in hope rather than imagine a life without Santa.

Alabaster led Olive away to fill up on food and to drink as much water as she could hold in her small stomach. When she was as full as could be he led her back to see Mrs. Claus.

"Are you ready, my sweet?" Mrs. Claus asked.

"Yes Grandmama, I'm ready," she said. The other reindeer gathered around to wish her a safe journey.

"I'm sorry I can't give you a blanket to keep you warm. It would only give you away."

"That's okay Grandmama. I'll be fine."

"I am going to sprinkle you with some magic fairy dust to help you fly farther, and I'll give you some to take with you. Use it sparingly as its effects wear down the more you use it. At the end of each day, allow the magic to regenerate by walking or resting."

Olive nodded.

"I'd give you more but there's not much left. Grandpapa Nick took most of it with him for his journey and the potion elves haven't been able to make more of it yet. Stay close to the ground so that you can save the magic. It will be easier to follow the terrain and see the lights from humankind towns. Unless you are in danger, stay away from humans."

"Why Grandmama? I thought everyone liked reindeer, especially Santa's flying reindeer."

"Those that believe in Santa would love to meet you but once people decide they don't believe, their minds change and they think all reindeer are the same. They will try to catch you."

"Oh dear!"

"They might even try to shoot you," Alabaster added.

"Whaaat?"

"Then try to eat you for supper!"

"Eat me?" she shrieked. "How awful!"

Mrs. Claus stroked Olive's neck. "They are not all bad and most people wouldn't eat you unless they were very hungry but it would be better to just stay away from them," she said soothingly.

"I think I will, Grandmama."

"Be careful of the polar bears as well. They will definitely want to eat you," Alabaster added.

"Oh." Olive felt sorry that she had been so eager to volunteer.

"And don't forget the wolves," Alabaster remarked, rolling up his map.

"W-wolves?"

"They hunt in packs and will tear you to shreds," Rollo said with a satisfied smirk.

"Oh, stop tormenting the girl, both of you!" Mrs. Claus scolded. "Don't you worry about what those two have to say, Olive. They are trying to scare you. You'll do just fine."

"But Grandmama Claus, what do I do if I do meet one of these...beasts?"

"If you face any one of these hunters, even humans, leap out of danger. They can't fly. Always keep your reindeer senses about you," she said putting on a brave face. She knew the others were quite right. This was indeed a dangerous mission indeed.

"Okay, Grandmama. We must find Papa," she said confidently with a look that said she meant business. "Which way do I go again?"

"You go that-a-way," they all said in unison, pointing south.

With that, Olive jumped into the air.

"Goodbye, Grandmama Claus," she shouted.

"Goodbye, little one," Mrs. Claus called after her.

"Goodbye everyone," Olive called to the others.

"Safe journey," Alabaster replied, biting his lower lip. The reindeer in the yard all raised their front hooves to wave good-bye.

Mrs. Claus watched until Olive was out of sight and sighed. "I sure hope we've done the right thing."

CHAPTER FIVE
Olive Finds Trouble

Even in the calm atmosphere inside the enchanted dome, Olive found her flight a little wobbly as she made her first long leaps in the air. With all the busy preparations for Christmas, it had been several weeks since her last flying lesson. And it showed.

"Whoa," she cried kicking her legs and trying to stay upright. With her hooves not touching the ground her balance was off causing her to swerve and tilt awkwardly first one way then another. "Oooops!" she squealed as she bumped into one of the ice peaks. To get used to flying and keeping her balance, she awkwardly leaned left then right, twisting her body to get the correct angle. When she tried to fly upward, she rolled completely upside down, spun around two more times, and then rolled back upright.

"Whoa, I'm not good with dizzy," she yelped as she did another spin. Her cries echoed across the entire enchanted dome before she got the knack of flying.

"What was that?" Mrs. Claus rushed to the window.

"What was what?" Alabaster asked without looking up from his mail desk.

"I thought I heard a shout."

"You must be hearing things, Mama Claus. I didn't hear a thing." Alabaster stood up and joined her at the window. They saw no sign of Olive, or anything else. Shrugging his shoulders, he went back to keeping himself busy during the nerve-wracking wait.

Olive felt quite woozy when she finally got herself upright and flying in a straight line and was soon skimming across the frozen ice with an awkward kind of competence.

"Whew! I should have paid more attention to my flying lessons with Papa and Grandpapa Nick," she muttered as she approached the rim of the enchanted dome. "No more playing games and not doing my homework!" she promised herself. She had never gone through the see-through wall before. "I hope this won't hurt," she cried out in anticipation. She closed her eyes, held her breath, and braced for impact but when she hit the wall she slipped through it without the slightest effort.

Wow! That was easy, she thought. *I didn't feel a thing!* Suddenly the cold winter winds whipped her and swirled and twirled her like a child's spinning top.

"Whoa!" she cried as the unexpected force swept her away, tumbling her over and over until she landed on the snow and ice. All four of her hooves splayed outward and she spun on the ice like a curling stone. It took all she had in her to dig her hooves in to stop spinning. "How do Grand Papa Nicholas and my Papa do this every year!" she cried, but no one heard her.

Digging her hooves in a patch of snow she managed to get back onto her feet, and then fighting the ferocious wind, she leapt once more into the air using all her might. She had to carry on and she hoped she was going the right direction. "Now I know what they mean when they said it was 'rough out here'!" she shouted but the howl of the wind snatched away the sound of her voice. Now she knew what her Papa meant when he talked about their long Christmas Eve journeys. "And cold! Now that's what I call cold!" she squealed, shaking. She had never experienced such bad weather before. "I can't feel my antlers or my nose or my hooves!"

With everything in her she wanted to turn around and go back to her warm stable. Then she heard Grandmama's voice in her head, 'Santa has not returned yet from his sleigh ride.' She knew she had to carry on to save Grandpapa Nick and her papa. "Olive," she declared, "this is not the time to be a coward!" She dipped her head and plunged once more into the bitter wind. "Full steam ahead!"

As time went on, fighting the storm sapped her energy. "This isn't going to be as easy as I thought," she puffed. "Not at all easy." Gradually though, she discovered that as she flew farther south, the winds began to die down and the night sky soon became crystal clear. With no sun rising at this time of year she could see the billions of stars overhead while the crystallized snow below her gave off a quiet, mysterious glow to light her way.

"Finally! Some decent weather a reindeer girl can get used to," she said, her self-assurance returning. "I think it's getting warmer too! It must be a balmy minus thirty degrees," she said, laughing at her own joke. She scanned the distance horizon looking for the lost team. "I can't see any sign of Papa, Grand Papa Nick, or the sleigh. No red, no sleigh, no antlers, nothing but this cold, white desert."

Now that the storm was behind her, Olive thought she had finally got the knack of flying and confidently decided to try a few moves. She swerved left then right, up then down. "Wheee," she squealed with delight. "This is wonderful! I feel free like a bird." She leapt up to perform a loop when out of nowhere a massive, white, fur-lined set of long claws reached out and swatted her to the ground.

Landing hard with an awkward thud, she shook her head. "What was tha…" Three reindeer leaps away, a huge roaring polar bear reared up on its haunches, its black eyes flashing.

"Yikes!" she screamed as she scrambled away.

"Not so fast!" the polar bear growled, placing her large paw on Olive's back and flattening the little reindeer on the snow.

"Do you mind?" Olive snapped. "You're squishing me!" She had never been hunted before and had no idea the trouble she was in.

"No I don't mind," answered the bear. "I like to flatten my meat like a schnitzel before I eat it."

"Eat it?" she yelped. "You mean me?" Instantly, terror rushed through her and she recalled Alabaster's warning.

"Do you see anyone else around?" the bear asked casually.

"But, but I'm a reindeer!" Olive protested, sweat beading on her forelock.

"Sounds tasty to me."

"But you can't eat me? I'm one of Santa's reindeer," Olive yowled.

"Santa? I know Santa. I like Santa," the bear mused. "He gives me treats for me and my cubs."

"You have cubs?" Olive hoped to distract the bear from trying to make a lunch out of her. Then she noticed two little white faces with dark eyes and black noses peering over a shard of ice, their white fur almost invisible against the sparkling snow.

"My name is Olive. What are your names?"

"Hey, wait a minute. What are you trying to do?" The bear placed another paw on Olive to hold her down.

"But, but you can't. I'm on a mission to save Santa. He's missing!"

"What? Santa is missing? Now come to think of it, I haven't seen him since he left some time ago."

"He's very late returning from his annual trip giving toys to all the little girls and boys around the world. Mrs. Claus sent me out to look for him."

The bear looked thoughtful. "I haven't seen him."

"We need Santa and I need to find him," Olive explained.

"I like Santa. You'd better go find him." The bear pulled her paw away from Olive's wriggling form.

"Thank you. I guess I'll be on my way."

"Sorry to have wanted to eat you for supper," the bear said, backing away.

"No problem…uh…"

"Agalu," the bear answered.

"What?"

"My name is Agalu. It means Tooth in your language," Agalu said, squatting on the snow. "And these are my cubs, Kunwaktok meaning smiles as he is always happy, and Agil meaning Yawn as she is always tired."

"Nice to meet you, Agulu, and Kunwaktok, and Agil," Olive replied. They ran up to play and scamper around her. Olive couldn't help but smile at the balls of white fluff bouncing in the snow. "You are so cute but I have to go and find Santa and my Papa and the rest of the reindeers."

The mama bear pulled her cubs away from Olive's feet. "You had better go before my stomach growls and I change my mind. I need to find food for these youngsters."

"I will make sure to let Santa know of your kindness, but now I need to head for the human settlement called Alert." With that Olive leapt into the air and headed into the dark.

"Where did you say you are going?" Agulu barked after her.

"I'm heading to Alert," Olive shouted over her shoulder.

"You need to go that-a-way." Agalu pointed her huge paw in a different direction.

"Oh, thank you," Olive said, swerving to change course.

That was a very nice bear, she thought as she once again headed south. *Everybody says polar bears are mean but Agalu was nice.*

At his post at the Canadian Forces radar station in Alert, a kitten by the name of Dickens, whose white paws looked like woollen mittens, sat on the lap of a young radar technician observing intently the mysterious blip on his screen. Waiting to pounce, Dickens lay ready for the golden dot to appear again and when it did, her paw shot out to catch the elusive point.

"There it is again! Captain sir, come look at my screen, there's a strange blip of a low flying object." He had never seen anything like it since they had tracked Santa and his reindeer heading south the day before.

"What was that, Corporal? Let me see," said the captain. The blip disappeared again. "I don't see anything."

"I saw it, sir, just like I did earlier," he insisted as Dickens jumped off his lap to find a less agitated place to curl up.

"Are you sure?" the Captain asked.

"Positive, sir. It was small but it was there."

"Well, keep an eye out. It could have been a stray bird or something."

"A bird? This far north?"

"Well, whatever it is make sure it isn't something important."

"Important?"

"Yes, like an invasion or something."

"Yes sir," the corporal replied, wondering how one little blip could be an invasion.

CHAPTER SIX
Is This the End of Christmas?

Santa awoke and drew a breath. All he could remember was that a massive ball of blue light had come barrelling up at the sleigh followed by a blinding flash.

What was that? Now fully conscious, Santa realized that he'd never seen such a thing before. His mind spun and he tried to shake his head. It was so confusing. Could it have been some kind of magic spell? A potion, a charm, or curse? If so, it was the most powerful spell he had ever seen.

Elves, wizards, and fairies all have their special spells and he had seen those from time to time but never anything like this. Even he had magic dust made by his Potion Elves. Somehow, though, this blue-tinged light seemed eerie and evil. It felt like something personal. He could make no sense of it.

He tried opening his eyes and found they were frozen shut. He sensed he was still holding the reins of the sleigh and he tried moving his arms and hands but they didn't budge even in the slightest. His legs were also frozen in place in the well of the sleigh. None of it made any sense.

This is so odd that I can't move, he thought, trying to squirm. *I seem to be trapped and frozen in place.* The more he struggled the more the immobilizing grip held. Fear crept over him for the first time in his mystical existence.

I hope my reindeer are okay, he thought.

"Dasher, Dancer, Prancer, Vixen, Comet, Cupid, Donner and Blitzen, are you okay?" he called out from the back of his throat because he could barely move his frozen lips. He could have sworn he heard a muffled cry but couldn't be sure.

"Rudolf, can you hear me?"

No response. *Oh dear, what am I to do?* he wondered. His next thought was for those he loved at the North Pole. A tear formed in his eye at the thought of not seeing his dear wife, Carol, the elves, and the younger reindeer ever again. Santa then thought about all the children who would be forever disappointed if he were never to return and spread the joy of Christmas; all those smiling faces of delight squealing at the wonderful surprises left under a decorated tree would turn sad.

I can't let this happen!

Santa struggled to open his eyes, straining with all his might. Finally, with a tiny flutter he was able to open them just a slit, barely enough to peep out. Around him, he could make out a pale blue glow that radiated brighter from his left and darker on the right. He felt cold, so very cold. Even with all his time living at the North Pole he had never felt such temperatures before. This was an evil chill that gripped him so tightly that no matter how much he tried it wouldn't let go. It was like he was suspended in a moment in time and place with no way out.

He stuck his tongue out from between his frozen lips just enough to touch the azure blue. It was solid ice. *How can this be?* He felt even more perplexed. *This must be a different ice than what I am used to at the North Pole. I don't freeze up there. Why am I frozen in ice here?*

Each of the reindeer was still harnessed to the sleigh and frozen in place exactly the same as Santa, suspended in mid-motion exactly like when the blue light had hit them. Dasher, through a blue haze, could see Rudolph's tail in front of him, and Dancer was frozen in place beside him. Prancer could see the murky tails of Dasher and Dancer beside him as did Prancer and Vixen, Comet and Cupid, and finally Donner and Blitzen but it was like looking through murky water and none of them could move so much as a hair.

Panicked thoughts raced through their heads. Where were they? What had happened? What was that strange blue light? Why couldn't they move? Because they could not turn their heads, no one knew if Santa was still behind them, or even if the sleigh was still attached.

They all knew they should be home by now and cozying up in their very own stalls on soft beds of straw. The elves would have lovingly brushed each reindeer down and would have had their favorite treats waiting for them upon their return. Fear crept through the ranks.

Was this the end of their magical story? Would they ever again fly with Santa on Christmas Eve? One by one, immense feelings of sadness overcame each reindeer. Would they ever see their loved ones back at the North Pole again? They knew that their cherished ones must all be terribly worried by now that they had not returned on time.

Meanwhile, Santa's began wondering how they could escape this frozen prison and if he might be able to use his magic shrinking dust. But it was in a pouch on his wide belt and no matter how much he tried to wriggle, there was no way he could reach it. With his arms frozen in place, he couldn't put his finger to his nose either in order to vanish like he did when there were chimneys, windows, and doors through which to escape.

Finally, he let out a big sigh. *Am I to be stuck here forever? Is this the end of Christmas?*

Santa closed his eyes again and reflected on the early days. Dasher and Dancer had been with Saint Nicholas since shortly after he started handing out gifts to the poor in Myra, Turkey, in the late third century. Before his parents had died, young Nicholas took to heart the lessons they and the monks who looked after him had taught him. He had learned it was always better to give than to receive. So Nicholas spent his inheritance helping the poor in any way he could. He collected food for needy people and made clothes and useful items, then he left the articles for them to find because he didn't want to be recognised. He knew he would be swamped with requests he could never hope to fill, so he quietly delivered his gifts at night when all were asleep and placed his offerings beside those with needs.

Once, when he was nearly discovered leaving gold coins for the dowries in the stockings of three motherless young girls, it was Dasher and Dancer who helped him to escape unseen. Over the years, Nicholas began putting an orange in the toe of the stockings to represent those first bags of gold to remind children of the same important message—it is better to give than to receive.

When he was young man, St. Nicholas worked many wonders, both large and small, around Europe for many disadvantaged people. From making a crutch for a lame child, or hand-carved wooden shoes for a Dutch boy, to a toy for a deserving child, he thought nothing of it. It gave him pleasure to do what he could to help people, especially the children.

Not only did he give gifts to the destitute and the little children, he also did many other good deeds. He prayed to calm rough seas, saving sailors on their voyage back from the Holy Land, and on another occasion, he rescued a slave boy from pirates.

Once his mortal life was over in year 352AD, he was declared a saint and allegedly given mystical powers to forever continue his good deeds…along with his reindeer friends.

Prancer and Vixen joined Bishop Nicholas as he travelled to Denmark where he became known as Sinter Klaus. All over Europe, as Father Christmas, he helped to feed the starving and give toys to children in their stockings to spread the Christmas spirit and honour the gifts of the Magi to the Christ child.

Comet and Cupid, Donner and Blitzen joined later when the toy bag grew larger and larger and he went farther afield to Iceland, Greenland, and New Amsterdam, the new world. There they knew him as Kris Kringle or Santa Claus. Now most young children now know him as Santa.

Rudolf was well over seventy years old when he joined the team, but he was the youngster in this experienced flying crew. Due to his bright red nose that shone both day and night, Rudolf was delighted when Santa asked him to join the team in 1939. A fog so dense it threatened to cancel Christmas had rolled in but Rudolf saved the night.

At first, when Santa asked Rudolf to join the crew, the other eight reindeer and their offspring were not impressed. After all, they had always guided Santa's sleigh on his annual epic journey and had handled the job very well for so many years. More than a little unsettled that the "new guy" was to be the lead reindeer, they were spiteful toward him, laughed at his bulbous nose, and called him names. Playing games with him was out of the question and so Rudolf was left alone in the reindeer playground.

As the senior reindeers of the team, Dasher and Dancer, didn't like their new view, especially after a long night of eating carrots and cookies! But all that changed on that foggy Christmas Eve when Santa asked Rudolf to guide his sleigh. From the front of the team, with his nose so bright he lit the way and saved Christmas. Santa was so relieved the children of the world would not be disappointed that he asked Rudolph to join the team permanently.

As they got to know him, the other reindeer saw that Rudolf had a big heart, was tremendously brave and had quickly learned where he was going around the whole world, which was difficult indeed. Even Dasher had to be reminded by Dasher every now and then which way to turn for their next stop, but Rudolf had done it on his first try.

Unlike the younger reindeer back at the stable, the older reindeer accepted Rudolf that very night and never laughed and called him names again. Since then Santa had used him many times and this night was no exception. Rudolf was in the lead once more trying to navigate through the dark and the bleak weather.

This time though, his red nose hadn't helped.

CHAPTER SEVEN
Alert

She had no way to know how tiring it was to fly, while at the same time concentrating on looking out for any sign her Papa, Grandpapa Nick, and the other reindeer. Barely staying awake, she decided it would be a good idea to land and rest for a little while to regain her strength, after all the wobbling and looping she had done. By slowing down, a rest would give the magic dust time to renew its powers.

After such a long day, it felt wonderful to have her hooves finally feel solid ice beneath her. There had been no signs of her papa and the team but thankfully, she hadn't seen any more polar bears either.

"Wow, I didn't think it would be this far," she said. "I'm exhausted." Papa only spoke about the stops in quaint towns and villages, smoggy cities, farm houses, and even tents and teepees, but never complained about how far it was between them all.

She missed the warm straw in her stable and being able to curl up snug as a bunny. Out here was only cold, and she realized how lucky she had always been to have a nice warm home and place to sleep each night without worry.

Olive wasn't hungry but she thought she might need to eat something to keep her strength up. She nuzzled the ground to see if there was anything to eat under the thick layer of snow. As she moved forward, she nudged what she thought was a bank of drifted snow. But instead, a creature leapt up into the air and bolted away like a rocket. "What was that?" she shrieked as she watched a pure white Arctic hare zigzag out of sight.

Wow, I must keep a sharper eye out, she thought, her heart racing and head swivelling. *It's a good thing that wasn't something more dangerous!*

She never knew that a hare could hide well in plain sight. "What other animals might be hiding out here in this wilderness?" she muttered, her natural senses now on high alert. From now on, she would have to carefully check an area before she landed. *If I am going to get through this, I am going to have to be more watchful; I'm not at the North Pole anymore!* Unsettled, she decided she didn't want to eat and nestled down against a snowdrift, away from the cold, to get some rest.

When she awoke, Olive had no idea how long she had slept but she felt rested, though sore from all the exercise she'd had the day before. Every muscle she had, or never realized she had, now complained miserably. It was a struggle simply to get up. Her legs and chest muscles protested with stiffness after her cold night on the ice. She also had no idea how far she had travelled on her first day. She had never practised long-distance flying in her beginner's flight training.

Olive could tell that the magic dust had regenerated and she felt a renewed spring in her step as she hopped into the air. She shook off the aches and complaints, deciding instead to concentrate on her mission. "I must get going if I am to find Santa and the rest of the team," she declared as she picked up speed.

Keeping a keen eye out for Grandpapa Nick and her Papa, Olive travelled on and soon worked out the kinks in her shoulders and hips, and by the time she neared Alert, she was flying with ease once again.

"Sir!"

The corporal in the Canadian Forces Station at Alert called to his captain. Dickens the kitten lay curled on his lap. "I see that blip again that I told you about yesterday," he said studying his radar screen.

"It can't be, we saw Santa's blip leaving two nights ago and there hasn't been any other scheduled flights," replied the captain peering at the monitor.

"See for yourself, sir. It's as plain as day. There's no identifier but something is out there."

"Yes, I see it, corporal. It sure is small. I don't think it's an aircraft." The captain scratched his head.

Dickens jumped up and with a white-mittened paw chased the little flashing lights on the screen.

"You don't think it's a missile, do you, sir?" the corporal asked, shooing Dickens away from the screen.

"I don't think so. It's travelling too slowly. It's not a drone either. Keep an eye on it and watch what it does, corporal."

"Yes, sir."

Olive saw the glow from the lights of Alert before she saw any of the buildings. As she got closer, she shouted, "Oh look, someone put up Christmas lights!" She saw multi-coloured strings of lights decorating the eaves of the buildings covered in a deep blanket of snow. "I like Christmas lights," she sighed fondly.

As she gazed below her, she recalled her instructions from Mrs. Claus. *Time to be turning right*, she thought as started to bank. Then she saw a white animal perched on one of the aerials at the top of a building. This required a closer look.

"That bird looks injured." Olive could see the bird's left wing drooping. *I hope its okay*, she thought, but then she saw that the bird couldn't take off as she approached. "I have to check this out," she whispered to herself. "She might need help," She descended and landed on the roof below where the bird perched.

"What was that?" the captain inside the building asked hearing the thump on the roof.

"Sounds like our UFO just landed," the corporal said. Dickens meowed in protest as he was shooed off the warm cozy lap.

"Well, we had better go up and take a look."

"Yes, sir. Thank goodness it wasn't a missile." The corporal grinned as he pulled on his parka. He had been at this northerly station long enough to know that if you weren't warmly dressed for the extremely cold weather a man could freeze to death in no time flat.

"I'll bring a rifle just in case," the corporal said reaching for his glasses.

Olive was about to ask the snowy owl if it was okay when a voice shouted from below.

"It's a reindeer!" the corporal hollered.

"How on earth did that get here?" replied the captain, standing near the open door. "Fly?"

"I'm sure the owl did, sir."

"No, I mean the reindeer!"

"It could be one of Santa's reindeer, sir. How else could it get here, if it wasn't one of Santa's reindeer?"

"Where are the rest of them?"

The corporal shrugged. "No idea, maybe she escaped."

"I've never heard of one of Santa's reindeer wanting to escape from the North Pole; not with all those goodies they get every year."

"Maybe she decided to go on a flight by herself."

"Where's Santa? I've never seen reindeer fly without Santa." The captain scratched is head. "I've seen them on radar. Maybe it's not one of Santa's reindeer."

"I've never seen Santa, let alone a flying reindeer," the corporal said.

"Nor have I, but I've seen them on radar," the captain replied.

"I thought I saw him once when I was a little boy," the corporal said scratching his head, "but I wasn't sure."

"Maybe it's not one of Santa's reindeer."

"Well it's not a drone or a missile," snickered the corporal. "We're still here." He breathed a little easier knowing it wasn't a spy drone or missile about to start the third world war.

"What was that you said, corporal?"

"Oh, nothing, sir. I was just wondering what else could it be?" he replied innocently, sending the captain a swift sideways glance.

"Well, what are we going to do with it?"

"I know what we shouldn't do, sir," the corporal said with a snort.

"What's that, corporal?"

"Report it, sir."

"Why not, soldier?"

"Let me see how the phone call will go, sir." He held his hand to his ear to mimic the captain reporting to his superiors. "'General, we report seeing a blip on the radar and discovered it was a flying reindeer. Yes sir, a flying reindeer. No, no, not a missile, space junk, and no, not a UFO or a drone either. We think it was one of Santa's reindeer. Yes that's right, General. One of Santa's reindeer." He mimed hanging up the phone.

"I see what you mean, corporal. Perhaps we won't report this after all," the captain agreed.

"Good idea, sir. I won't log it either." The corporal climbed down from the rooftop. "I like being part of 'The Frozen Chosen' team but my posting is up in a month and I get to go to somewhere warm. I really want to go somewhere warm, sir."

"Do you think we should shoot it and have some reindeer meat in the freezer?"

"I wouldn't, sir. If it is one of Santa's reindeer, I wouldn't want to be the one to get a piece of coal in my stocking every Christmas for the rest of my life."

"You have a point there, soldier."

"I think we should forget about the whole thing, sir."

"Good idea, corporal. Let's go back inside and have a cup of cocoa and watch a movie," the captain suggested.

"Rudolf the Red Nosed Reindeer, sir."

The captain laughed. "I don't think so. How about *The Christmas Carol*, the 1951 version with Alistair Sim That's one of my favorite movies. It always puts me into the spirit of Christmas."

"Sounds good to me, Captain, sir." They never spoke of the incident ever again.

CHAPTER EIGHT
Chloe the Snowy Owl

"Well, that was strange," Olive said after seeing humankind other than Grandpapa and Grandmama for the first time. "I wonder if they always act that way?"

"You'll never figure whoomans out, whoot hoot," the owl answered.

"You speak!" Olive exclaimed. "How nice."

"I'm called Chloe the Snowy Owl by all my friends, whoot hoot." Chloe chirped so rapidly the words were a jumble.

"Nice to meet you, Chloe the Snowy Owl. My name is Olive. Where did you learn to speak?"

"Never underestimate a wise old owl with experience, whoot hoot," the owl said proudly fluffing up her chest feathers. "You can usually dodge a question with a long-winded answer."

"Okay then, how did you get here?"

"Someone once said that experience is a wonderful thing. It lets you recognise a mistake when you make it again," Chloe hooted. "I thought I'd try something different. Have you ever attempted to do something different? Whoot hoot."

"I am trying to be a flying reindeer!" This was all Olive could think of. "Maybe I can lead Santa's sleigh one day just like my papa."

"And how's that going for you? Whoot hoot."

"Well…"

"I know exactly what you mean. You know, trying to outsmart the competition, whoot hoot."

"Well, not really. We are all friends up at the North…"

Chloe interrupted. "There is only so much food to go around up in the tundra so I thought I'd try going north instead of south for the winter. You know, become an adventurist, be brave, seek new worlds, and all that jazz. What a mistake! I had never flown this far north before so I didn't know how freezing it was until I got here. Definitely too frosty for my feathers, whoot hoot."

This bird talks a lot, Olive thought. "How did you hurt your wing?"

"It was dark and stormy night and as I flew farther north it became colder and colder until my wings got so cold they froze up and I couldn't move them anymore to steer. Just as I was about to make a controlled crash landing, to my surprise straight out of the dark, I saw this herd of nine hairy creatures looking just like you, pulling a red sleigh with a jolly whoomankind in a red suit riding in the back and coming straight toward me, whoot hoot."

"That must have been Santa on his way to deliver toys on Christmas Eve!" Olive said doing a little dance.

"Those beasts were wild-eyed, snorting, clipping and a clopping, jingling and jangling along and heading straight for me, whoot hoot.

"'Those beasts you mention are reindeer, and my papa was one of them," Olive announced proudly.

"I didn't have time to introduce myself," the owl countered. "It was all a blur to me, whoot hoot."

"No worries. Then what happened?" Olive asked.

"This jingling thing was coming straight for me. Frozen like I was, I couldn't get out of the way. I tried to pull up to miss them and if I weren't as stiff as a board I would have made it. I can fly very well, I don't mind telling you."

"I'm sure you can."

"I barely managed to miss the sharp points of the reindeer antlers, the red cap on the whoomankind too, but then I flew straight into one of the huge bags stacked high in your, what do you call him…Santa's sleigh, whoot hoot." Chloe winced when she tried moving her wing.

"Oh dear, I'm so sorry to hear that happened to you. Are you in much pain?"

"Without pain we don't learn pleasure, whoot hoot," Chloe hooted sadly.

"I'm shocked that Santa didn't stop?"

"It was snowing so hard that not even I, with my marvellous owl vision, could see anything in that mess, whoot hoot. I don't think the whoomans realized I had hit the overstuffed sack. He had just taken off from the roof of one these huts in the village yelling, 'Ho, Ho' Ho'! Whoot hoot."

"Oh dear," Olive said again.

"He was travelling so fast I think he was flying at the speed of dark, whoot hoot!" Chloe chirped rapidly. "There should be a speed limit when he's in towns. He might hit something, whoot hoot!"

"Don't you mean the speed of light?"

"Well, it was dark at the time, whoot hoot!"

"I'm sure he would have stopped if he had known you were hurt."

"I don't trust whoomans. None of us owls or any forest animal do, whoot hoot."

"Oh, I know Santa would have for sure," Olive answered, nodding vigorously. "He's kind and gentle and loves all the animals, big and small, fierce and tame. I'm sure he would have fixed you up in no time. Is there anything I can do to help?"

"I don't know what you can do. I'll just stay here and rest until the weather warms up and I can fly again, whoot hoot."

"It's the middle of winter so that could take months. By then you'll probably starve to death."

"Or freeze to death, it won't matter which, whoot hoot," Chloe said sadly, as though resigned to her fate. "It's the way of nature, you know, whoot hoot."

"We can't let that happen," Olive said firmly. "I'm not going to let you freeze to death up here if I can help it."

"What do you suggest?" Chloe asked, hope in her voice for the first time. "There's nowhere warm for me to perch around here unless I go into one of the whoomankind nests and I'm not going to fly into one of them."

"At least it would be warm for you."

"Out of the frozen pot and into the fire, whoot hoot!"

"What do you mean?"

"They have already captured a cat and pointed a bang stick at you, whoot hoot," Chloe said blinking one of her big golden eyes. "What do you think they will do to me?"

"Hmmm, my Grandmama told me not to trust humans as well." She perked up. "I have an idea! I'm heading south so if you would like, you can ride with me until you feel better. I have found out I'm not very good with directions so maybe we can help each other out."

"That sounds just fine. Thank you, whoot hoot." Chloe gave a quavering laugh.

"Do you think I might get lost occasionally?"

"No, no. Think of it, a snowy owl riding on the back of a flying reindeer. Tell me, where in the world have you heard of that before? Whoot hoot."

"Why, never."

"Exactly, whoot hoot." Both animals giggled as Chloe hopped onto Olive's back and perched on her shoulders. Olive took a few hops, then lifted off.

"Which way is south?" Olive asked.

"That-a-way," Chloe said, pointing with her good wing.

"Oh, right," Olive said over her shoulder and corrected her course.

As Grandmama had advised, they followed the coast of Ellesmere Island and other smaller coastal islands, which were almost impossible to tell apart with the arctic ice still covering both the Arctic Ocean and the islands.

"I can't tell you how thankful I am for the ride, whoot hoot," Chloe said, clinging to Olive's back.

"Don't mention it," Olive replied sincerely. "I feel bad about what it happened to you. I hope your wing will be better soon."

"I *must* mention it. Someone once told me not to forget that appreciation is always appreciated, whoot hoot." Chloe twittered.

"Where do you get these sayings?"

"I couldn't be a wise owl if I didn't have wise sayings could I, whoot hoot?"

"Er, I guess you're right," Olive mused.

They crossed Nansen Sound and flew onto the coast of Axel Heiberg Island where they saw few animals. Olive remembered her experience with the Arctic hare so she knew animals could be there anyway. They soared over the McGill Arctic Research Station with little to be seen but snow. The outpost appeared all but deserted but there again, the humans could all be hunkered down inside warm huts and out of this cold. The one thing Olive didn't see was any sign of Santa, her papa, or the sleigh.

Eventually, more and more barren land started poking out from under the ice. There were no humankind settlements on these barren lands but she saw countless colonies of arctic animals.

"Whoot hoot, why are you out here flying, Olive?" Chloe asked.

"I'm on a mission to find Santa and the rest of the reindeer team, including my papa," she replied.

"That sounds serious. What happened? Whoot hoot."

"We are not sure. When he didn't come back from delivering the toys to all the children, Grandmama Claus sent me out to find him."

"That sounds like a very important mission; she must put a lot of trust in you, whoot hoot,"

"I guess so. I am very happy she chose me." Olive thought of Rollo and felt proud of herself.

"Where did you say you were from?"

"From the North Pole."

"The North Pole? There's a nest way up there? Whoot hoot."

"Oh yes, there's a house actually, elf bunkhouse, a toy warehouse and factory, and a warm cosy stable for us reindeer. It's a place I would really love to be right now."

"There is no place like home sweet home where the reindeer roam and you can put up your feet and let down your feathers, whoot hoot."

As they flew onward, they could see some of the animals that make their homes in the arctic. First, a pod of walrus rose through a breathing hole in the ice. They lounged in the fresh air and basked on the ice close by the hole so they could make a quick escape if a nosy polar bear should come around.

Next, two narwhal appeared in another pool after they had broken through the surface ice with their long unicorn-like horns. Later on, they saw a herd of muskoxen foraging for food on the barren rock. All this was a true wonderment for Olive, who was seeing all these things for the first time. But her enjoyment was clouded, as there were still no signs of Santa, the team, or the sleigh. Olive missed her papa, Prancer, most of all.

"Have you seen any other animals on your journey? Whoot hoot" Chloe asked, breaking the silence.

"I met a giant polar bear and her cubs just after I left the enchanted curtain. Her name was Agalu."

"A polar bear, yikes! Did she hurt you? Whoot hoot!"

"No not at all. She was nice to me."

"Nice? I've never heard of a nice polar bear. They like to eat meat, including the likes of me and you, whoot hoot."

"I was scared at first when she swatted me out of the air…"

"Swatted?" Chloe interrupted. "You mean with one of those gigantic paws full of claws they have? Whoot hoot."

"Yes, but…"

"And you're still in one piece, whoot hoot?"

"When she found out about my mission to save Santa, her mood changed right away because somehow she knew who Santa was and likes him."

"Why would a polar bear like a whooman? Whoot hoot."

"I guess he gives her treats every now and then when he passes through from the Pole," she said eagerly. "I even met her white, fluffy cubs Kunwaktok and Agil."

"A polar bear with cubs! Now I know this is one strange bear.

"I think Agalu is such a nice polar bear. "

"I think she must be a bi-polar bear. Whoot hoot."

CHAPTER NINE
Sly

"I sure hope Olive is okay," a worried Mrs. Claus muttered, pacing back and forth across the kitchen floor.

"I'm sure she is," Alabaster replied entering the room and trying to console them both by keeping his voice calm. Inside, though, he was worried, too.

"No news is good news, I guess." Mrs. Claus attempted to put on a brave appearance in front of all the other elves.

The dark Christmas tree stood alone in the corner of the living room with all the unopened gifts lying under it untouched. Without their loved ones, the cosiness of the room and the magic of Christmas had all faded away. Oh, the fireplace still crackled and popped but it didn't feel the same without the anticipation of Santa's return. His overstuffed chair usually glowed in the dancing firelight but now looked glum without the prospect of its owner napping comfortably within its embrace.

Rather than facing the emptiness, no one ventured into the living room even to shake a present or two. The mood had indeed changed completely. Mrs. Claus wondered if the joy of Christmas would ever come back. The big question everybody was afraid to ask was if their beloved

Nicholas and the reindeer would ever return, safe and sound. They took turns wandering to the windows only to stare blankly off into the deep blue of the arctic distance.

"I have sent word out to all the Santa helpers, shopping mall Santas, gnomes, tooth fairies, regular fairies, and even elves on shelves to keep an eye out for both Santa and Olive," Alabaster said trying to put a positive spin on the situation. He too had seen and felt the once glorious living room turn into some kind of sad reminder of what was, rather than a happy place to gather.

"Oh, thank you, Alabaster. What would I do without you?"

"The magic cat, Dickens—you know the kitten with white woollen mittens at the Alert Station—has just reported that she saw Olive on the radar screen," Sprinkles cried rushing in from the mailroom.

"Finally! Some good news!" Alabaster shouted.

"She landed on the roof of the radar hut early this morning," Sprinkles added, out of breath.

"On the roof! The humans didn't get her did they?" Mrs. Claus asked, surprised to hear that Olive hadn't followed her instructions.

"No, no they didn't want to believe what they saw so they just pretended it didn't happen," Sprinkles reported with a giggle.

"What was she doing on the roof? I told her to be wary of humankind. She could have got herself hurt or captured," Mrs. Claus cried.

"Or killed!" Alabaster added.

"Oh hush, Alabaster! I won't hear of such talk. We must stay positive," Mrs. Claus admonished sternly.

"Yes, Grandmama," they answered contritely.

"Is there any other news?" Mrs. Claus asked. "Anything at all?"

"I'm afraid not, Grandmama Claus. Dickens reported seeing Santa's blip on the screen on Christmas Eve but hasn't seen his return."

"Well, that tells us something at least. He didn't crash land in the Arctic."

"There's been nothing reported back from any of the other sources," Sprinkles added.

"Not a thing?"

"Not one word."

"Oh dear," Mrs. Claus replied, sinking into her flowered armchair.

"Don't worry, Mama Claus, it's still early yet. Hopefully we'll hear from someone else soon," Alabaster said, trying to lift the mood. "One of the reindeer at least will make it back and let us know where the rest are."

"Olive will find them," she replied. "I'm sure of it." She hoped her words encouraged the others, but in fact, she wasn't sure at all.

By this time, Olive and her passenger were flying over Melville Island. Below, they saw more large, hairy muskoxen roaming the treeless land. Immense flocks of arctic terns huddled on rocks and cliffs, or floated on the cold air currents that came before storms blew in. Large cracks appeared in the ocean ice. As Olive and Chloe approached Banks Island they noticed immense slabs of ice floating freely in the even bigger Beaufort Sea.

It was Chloe who first noticed the tall dorsal fins and spraying spouts of mist breaking the water's surface. Before long they both spotted the telltale black and white bodies arc up and back into the water, flukes flipping high in the air. There was no doubt this was a pod of orcas, or killer whales.

"Whoot, whoot! Danger, danger! Killer whales, killer whales! Whoot hoot!"

"Yes, I see them Chloe. Boy, are they ever big!" she observed. "There must be five or six of them," Olive steered downward for a closer look.

"Fear has a magnifying glass that makes a beast look bigger and meaner than he really is. Whoot hoot!"

"Yes but these things are huge!"

"Don't get too close. They'll give you a whale of a time and not in a fun way! Whoot hoot" Chloe shrieked.

"It looks like they are surrounding one slab of ice, I wonder why?" Olive managed to say just before she saw one of the Orcas skidding up onto the slab to snare a seal.

"Whoa! Is it a game they are playing?"

"There is little time for games in the wilderness, Miss Olive. Whoot hoot!"

The whale's gaping mouth, lined with huge teeth, appeared to sink its bite into something trapped at one end of the ice floe. The other five hungry hunters circled the island to ensure their intended meal didn't escape their waiting grasp.

The floating ice slab tilted heavily under the weight of the huge orca hunting its prey. Whatever was on the ice skidded toward the gaping jaws of the cunning hunter.

"It looks like that orca planned that," Olive observed, staying out of range.

"Killer whales are masters of planning. Failing to plan is planning to fail, whoot hoot."

The prey on the ice surface scrambled frantically to hold on and stop its slide. Somehow it managed to cling to the slippery surface and pull itself back up to safety just in time.

The whale, having failed in the attack, slid back into the water causing the ice slab to bob up and down. The terrified creature skittered to the opposite edge, frantically searching for an escape route but it was trapped on the small raft of ice. The other orcas circled the ice, waiting for another chance and making sure there was no escape route.

"What is that on the ice?" Olive squinted for a better look. "It's white, furry, and so small!"

"I believe it's their supper, whoot hoot!"

"That is hardly a meal for all those whales," Olive observed. "A nibble for one at best."

"I prefer thawed to frozen dinners, whoot hoot!"

"Don't remind me that you eat meat! I'm sure you wouldn't want to be whoever that is on the ice, even if it is just a snack," Olive snapped.

"True, although I'm sure I would only get stuck between its teeth, whoot hoot!"

"I don't want to see it get stuck between anyone's teeth. We have to try to help," Olive stated.

"The whale? Whoot hoot!"

"No! Whoever is on the ice."

"Don't get too close, whoot hoot! You'll be a lot more of a supper than the scrawny appetiser they are hunting now!"

Olive swooped down and hovered above the ice until she recognized the animal. It was an Arctic fox.

"Whoot hoot, a fox, a fox, a fox!" Chloe hooted excitedly, "Why did it have to be a fox? Whoot hoot."

"Oh, don't get so excited. He looks so cute!"

"Whoot hoot, cute, cute! He's not cute! That sneaky beast hunts and eats birds and their eggs! Whoot hoot."

"Oh, I didn't realize. I'm a vegetarian. We still have to try to save him." Unwittingly Olive now hovered just above the water, unaware of how killer whales hunt.

Without warning one of the orcas breached out of the ocean and lunged toward a leaping Olive. "Whoa," she yelled as she narrowly escaped the snapping bite.

"You can survive almost anything except death! Whoot hoot!" Chloe screeched fluttering her wings and clinging for dear life to Olive's back.

Olive learned quickly the exact distance above the water she had to stay to avoid the ever-watchful hunters. As Chloe had predicted, they had turned their interest on her. At the same time she cunningly tried drawing them away from the stranded fox by gliding down close enough to the water surface to entice the whales to chase her then, amidst Chloe's frantic hooting and desperate protest, bounding up just in time as they lurched out of the water for the chance of a quick dinner.

When she thought she had lured them far enough away, she turned and raced as fast as she could to the slab of floating ice and landed on it, with the pod of whales in hot pursuit. What she hadn't known was that the first killer whale she had seen, perhaps the pod leader, had stayed just under the surface of the water waiting for such a move.

Suddenly, the gigantic orca flung his body up onto the ice floe and squirmed and flipped toward Olive and the arctic fox. The gaping jaws with their rows and rows of gleaming, sharp teeth snapped at her.

Olive screamed and leapt away from the enormous, menacing marauder.

Both Olive and the fox backed away as far as they could while the whale wriggled intently toward them. At the very edge of the ice, about to be pushed into the frozen ocean, the whale's enormous weight tipped the ice slab, flipping it over end over end. The orca slid back into the deep while Olive and the fox flew through the air and splashed into the freezing sea.

Chloe flapped her wings frantically and hopped onto Olive's antlers as she tried to stay above water.

"Holy Christmas! This is cold!" Olive yelled, up to her neck in the water.

"Whoot hoot! Whoot hoot! Look out, look out, danger, danger!" Chloe screeched as the rest of the whales bore down on them. The fox and Olive frantically thrashed about in the sub-zero sea trying to stay afloat. Chloe, still squawking for all she was worth, hopped up onto the very tip of Olive's tallest antler.

Olive saw the tell tale dorsal fins approach with determined swiftness. She knew she and her new friends were in deep trouble and she had to think of something and fast.

The orcas could sense success as they closed in with the excitement of the hunt. Water sprayed like geysers from their blowholes as the pod surged on sounding like a steam engine shunting out of a railway station. But when they got close they suddenly slipped eerily under the surface.

"Where did they go?" Olive's eyes frantically skimmed the surface of the water around her.

"They're coming from underneath for a final attack, Whoot hoot!" Chloe squawked.

"Jump on my back," Olive ordered the fox, "and do it quickly!"

The frantic fox paddled to his rescuer's side and managed to claw his way onto her back. As soon as she felt the fox safely upon her, Olive used all her might to leap out of the frigid water. But the cold had taken its toll on her muscles causing them to react much slower than she expected, and she didn't quite make it. With another mighty, strained effort she kicked her legs and slowly pulled her freezing body out of the clinging drag of the icy sea and into the air. The gaping jaw of the first returning hunter breached out of the dark green sea and snapped shut behind her, narrowly missing her rear hoof.

"Whoot hoot! Whoot hoot" Chloe squealed feeling the breath of the great beast blast her.

Olive's heart was racing. She tried to gain more height. Just then another orca broke high out of the water in a final attempt to snatch her out of the air. She tucked up her hind legs then kicked as hard as she could and caught the unsuspecting orca in the jaw. The startled whale snarled as it splashed back into the sea.

"That was scary!" Olive cried out when she knew she was in the clear.

"You had just the right amount of fear to succeed, whoot hoot!" Chloe hooted.

"What do you mean, oh, wise one?"

"Fear can make fools of two other kinds of animals: the one who is afraid of nothing and the other nothing but afraid. Both will get them killed, whoot hoot!"

Olive landed on the shore of Banks Island far enough inland that the waiting orcas could not reach them, but

Olive could see their menacing fins pacing back and forth just off shore.

"Every day I run scared. That's how I stay alive," said the fox, jumping down from Olive's back.

"Then you, too, have just the right amount of fear to succeed, whoot hoot," Chloe whooped staying high up on Olive's antlers, as far away as possible from the untrustworthy fox.

"Thank you, reindeer, for being so quick. I thought I was gonna be their supper for sure," the fox said. "I'm truly grateful."

"You are more than welcome. I just reacted, really."

"You were no meal. You were a training toy for the young killers, whoot hoot."

"Either way, I was a goner until you guys showed up."

Olive saw how skinny the fox was with his fur wet and could still see the fear still in his eyes. "Are you okay?" she asked him.

"I think so. Nothing a little warmth won't fix." Ice crystals were forming at the tips of the fur of both the fox and Olive and both began to shiver.

"Fear may slow down our thinking but sure does speed up our footwork!" Chloe observed. "Whoot hoot!"

"By, by, the, the way m-m-my name is O-O-Olive and this is Ch-Chloe. Wha-wha-what's yours?" she said through chattering teeth.

"M-m-my name is rather co-co-common really, I-I-I'm called Sly, Sly Stone, the Fox."

"Whoot hoot! If I heard anything so true, that fits! You guys are always sneaking around stealing stuff, like our eggs!" Chloe scolded.

"Oh hush, Chloe. It's in their n-nature," Olive said, shaking off ice crystals and feeling a little warmer. "Hunters like you can't help but eat meat. Don't you hunt creatures like mice and lemmings?"

"I don't eat somebody's precious eggs! Whoot hoot!"

"Okay, okay I get it; we foxes always get the blame. My cousin the Red Fox got us the bad rep because his favourite meal is chickens. Everybody likes chickens so all of us foxes are the bad guys. That's why we had to learn to trust no one and sneak around and stay out of sight," Sly said, hanging his head and slinking away.

"Where are you going?" Olive asked after him.

"I thought you didn't want me around."

"No, no don't be silly. Don't listen to Chloe. I'm sure she isn't a favorite with the lemmings either but that's the way life is."

"I really do want to thank you for saving my life. I was lucky you came along at the right time," Sly said in earnest as he happily returned. "I will appreciate it for the rest of my life, however long that is in this unforgiving and endless winter," Sly replied.

"You'll live longer if you stay away from the ocean, whoot hoot!" Chloe chirped.

Olive laughed. "I think we should rest here before we carry on with our journey." She suddenly felt tired from all the excitement, "We can get dry and warm together."

"A good way to forget your own troubles is to help others with theirs, whoot hoot!" Chloe observed.

Olive found a patch of tundra moss amongst the gravel in the barren landscape, circled twice and made a makeshift nest. Once snuggled down she asked, "How did you get out there in the first place?"

"I was chasing a scent," Sly said.

Chloe gasped.

"No, not a bird!" he said. "I didn't realize I had gotten onto the sea ice and before I knew it, it broke away from the icepack and I was stuck. I was hoping it would float back to shore with the tide but the orcas discovered me first and pushed the ice slab out to deeper water. I thought I was done for."

"Those crafty fish," Olive said, understanding that orcas hunt with a plan.

"Orcas are mammals, not fish, whoot hoot!"

"Okay, crafty mammals then. They are cunning."

"They hunt in packs like wolves," Sly said. He had had several close calls with the local pack of arctic wolves.

"Wolves?" Olive looked around nervously.

"Yes, they're around, so always keep one eye open for them at all times," Sly warned. "That's what I do. White Storm is the leader of the pack around here."

"Oh dear," Olive sighed, "just when I thought we were safe."

"You are never safe in the wilderness but here the muskoxen keep them at bay as do the humankind."

"Humankind? Are there humankind nearby?"

"The hunters. They hunt by sea and by land for a living, and live south of here in a small village they call Sachs Harbour," Sly explained. "But I stay away, far away, from them and I advise that you do the same."

"I think I will, too," Olive said remembering what Grandmama and Alabaster had warned her about the humankind.

CHAPTER TEN
Onward

The night was bitterly cold, chilling to the bone, and rough on the fur after the freezing winds had come back in the evening and stayed throughout the night. By morning another layer of unwelcomed ice crystals, sprayed by the wind from the sea, had sprinkled them like a blanket of icing sugar on a doughnut.

To stay warm, they had all snuggled together tucked in next to Olive. Even Chloe had nestled herself next to Sly because of his thick fur, but being the untrusting and suspicious owl she was, and knowing what foxes can be cunning little creatures, had kept one golden eye open all night just in case.

Sly was grateful for the shelter and slept all night peacefully, without a single blink. Using Olive as a windbreak to prevent heat loss, the arctic fox curled up tightly, tucking his legs and head under his body and behind his furry tail.

Olive, on the other hand, hardly slept. She was constantly worried about her papa and Grandpapa Nicholas and hoped with all her might she wouldn't be too late. She wanted to find them all safe and sound.

"Gooooooood morning, guys," Sly said cheerfully when he woke, up stretching his front legs.

His tired and bleary-eyed travelling companions answered with weary groans.

"Are you guys okay? I slept like a black bear in hibernation!" Sly said watching Olive yawn and stretch. "Wow, I feel greeeaaaat! I haven't slept that well in years. Thanks Olive, for the cozy bed," he said.

"You're welcome," Olive moaned keeping her eyes closed, hoping for few more minutes of sleep.

"Whoot hoot, I should have counted my sheep in twos then maybe I would have fallen asleep faster," Chloe grumbled.

"I know the reason I am here is because I live here. But why are you guys here?" Sly asked after they had stood up and shaken off the layer of morning snow.

"Well, Chloe is here because she went north instead of south for the winter…"

Chloe interrupted. "Excuse me, I like to see it as a positive thing like an experiment, an adventure, or nothing ventured nothing gained kind of thing rather than a negative. Unfortunately, I ran into the whooman called Santa and his sleigh, literally, and hurt my wing, whoot hoot."

"Santa's sleigh?" Sly quizzed. "You mean the real Santa in the red suit and lives in the North Pole?"

"Yes, I believe so. That's who Olive said he was anyway. I have never seen him myself. Whoot hoot."

"How could you not see Santa's sleigh? It's big enough."

"Whoot hoot! I actually missed the sleigh and ran into the bag of toys. It's rather a long story and…"

"Wow, you actually saw him. How lucky you are!"

"I guess you could say that but my wing doesn't think so. Whoot hoot."

"But you saw Santa!"

"That's why I'm here," Olive said.

"You are…why are you here?" Sly turned to Olive.

"I'm searching for Santa and my papa."

"Aren't we all? Not for my papa but I have searched for Santa for as long as I have lived and never seen him," Sly said, dancing around.

"No, I mean I am searching for him because he didn't come back to the North Pole Christmas morning and Grandmama Claus sent me out to look for him. You haven't seen him, have you?"

"Er, as a matter of fact I haven't. But what do you mean you were sent out to look for him?"

"Well, I'm one of Santa's reindeer…"

"In training, whoot hoot," corrected Chloe.

"Yes, in training. And I…"

"You are one of Santa's reindeer?" Sly's eyes widened.

"Well, technically, no. I am the daughter of Prancer but I am in training in hopes to become one someday."

"Well, I'll be. I slept with one of Santa's reindeer," Sly said, grinning. "I can't wait to tell my family about this. They'll be so excited."

"I'm not sure I'd put it that way," Olive suggested.

"It's a pity that happiness isn't as easy to find as trouble is, whoot hoot," Chloe commented.

"I guess you're right." Sly gave the owl a strange look. "So what do you think happened?" he asked Olive.

"We don't know if he crashed, got grounded with bad weather, or it was something worse such as lying somewhere unconscious. All we know is that he didn't return and no one has seen him since he left Christmas Eve."

"I hope the Blizzard Wizard didn't get him."

"What do you mean? Who is the Blizzard Wizard?"

"Oh, you don't want to cross paths with the Blizzard Wizard. He's real mean-spirited and will freeze you like a icicle just for looking at him."

"Oh my, I hope he didn't get Santa," Olive cried.

"Someone said that 'hatred freezes hearts, while love warms them.' Whoot hoot " Chloe added.

"Yes, he hates everything and everyone and he roams these parts stirring up storms all the time and causing all kinds of trouble. He probably started the storm we had last night and the one the night before that."

"Where do you think he came from?"

"Some say he's an old sea captain who froze to death on Christmas Day many years ago. I stay away, far away."

"I think we will, too. Let's hope Santa only crash landed somewhere," Olive replied.

"While we breathe, there's always hope, whoot hoot."

"Where did you get this guy?" Sly asked frowning at Chloe.

"Owls are supposed to be wise," Olive explained.

"I'm not sure if she is wise or just a wise guy…er girl." It was clear Chloe's proverbs were starting to annoy him.

"Chloe is just trying to help, in her own way."

"Criticism says more about the person giving it than receiving it, whoot hoot," Chloe commented, ruffling up her feathers.

Realising that owls and foxes do not make the best of companions, Olive distracted them. "You are more than welcome to come with us, and when we find Santa I will introduce you to him."

"Thank you for the offer, and please don't take offense because I would really love to meet Santa, but I need to get back to my family. Mrs. Stone and the kits are counting on me," Sly replied. "And I still need to find some food for us."

"Whatever you wish," Olive said. "As long as you're okay,"

"I promise not to go over the sea ice ever again." Sly crossed his heart with his paw.

"Farewell. I hope we will see each other again one day," Olive said then jumped up into the air and started flying east.

"That would be nice. I will look forward to it. Farewell and safe journeys," Sly called after her, waving with one paw.

"Are you sure you want to go this way, whoot hoot," Chloe asked, peering down into Olive's left eye.

"Am I not going south?"

"Whoot hoot, no way, no way."

"Which way is south?"

"That-a-way," Sly called pointing south.

As Sly disappeared from sight, Olive said, "I hope Sly and his family Stone will be safe."

Now that she was out of the fox's range, Chloe had warmed to her natural enemy. "Me too, Olive, me too."

With Chloe on her back, Olive stayed on the route Santa would have taken, keeping to the shoreline of Banks Island and flying low to avoid being seen. She knew at some point she would need to turn in a south-westerly direction but she couldn't see anything but ice and the vast open ocean to the west. *If Grandpapa Nick and the reindeer went down in there, there's no way anyone would find ever them*, she thought.

It didn't take long before Olive saw her first fishing boat patrolling the open waters off to the west, then another came into view, and another. With her keen eyesight, Chloe was able to see the boats long before they got close to them. She recognized that none were Santa and the reindeer floating in the ocean and reported to Olive. They flew on, leaving the bobbing crafts to the will of the waves.

Several more fishing boats appeared as she headed into the gulf between Banks Island and the mainland of the Canadian Northwest Territories. All seemed quiet until they reached the midpoint of the strait when Olive heard something buzz by her ear.

"What was that?" she asked Chloe.

"I did not know there were arctic bees buzzing around up here, whoot hoot." Chloe replied her head spinning around.

"I've never seen a bee before, especially an arctic bee," Olive admitted. Just then another whizzing sound passed her followed by a loud bang.

"What was that!?" she screeched.

"I believe that was a bullet we heard buzz past us, whoot hoot!" Chloe hooted. She had heard that sound before.

"A bullet! Yikes! Like from a gun?"

"I believe so. I think whooman fire sticks are shooting at us, whoot hoot!" Chloe flapped her wings in panic.

"Let's get out of here fast!" Olive screamed, diving toward the surface to skim across the icy water. She hoped to make Chloe and herself harder target to hit.

"Are you kidding me? Whoot hoot," Chloe yelped as another bullet clipped a tail feather. She leaped up onto Olive's antlers.

Olive could see the muzzle flashes coming from a boat off to her right and decided to swerve left, then right, and then to veer left again as deer would do naturally when running away on solid ground. Terrified, Olive's natural instincts took over as she darted one way then another as more bullets flew past them.

"Whoot hoot, slow down. I think you can stop tearing around now," Chloe hooted.

"What do you mean 'slow down'?" Olive shouted. "We've got to get away from all those bullets!"

"The bang bangs have stopped, whoot hoot."

"What?"

"The bangs from the whoomankind guns have stopped, whoot hoot," Chloe assured her.

Only when Olive realized that indeed the pops and cracks had stopped did the panic in her eyes, the hammer noise in her head, and her rapid panting begin to ease. She stopped zigzagging and gradually slowed down from her mad gallop to a more typical pace. She needed to stop and catch her nervous breath and let her pounding heart slow down so she chose a spot and landed on the barren landscape of the tundra.

Remembering what Grandmama Claus had said, she knew she had used a lot of energy to escape being shot and had used too much of her magic dust.

"I need to conserve the magic," she said as she came to a stop. "I don't want to have to start walking." She turned her head around to check on her friend. "Are you okay Chloe?"

"I got my feathers ruffled a bit if that's what you're asking, whoot hoot."

"But you're bleeding!" Olive responded, seeing a trickle of blood seep down her sagging wing.

"Bleeding? Where? Whoot hoot." Chloe began checking her body, lifting her feet, and craning her neck to check her tail.

"Your injured wing has a hole in it."

Chloe twisted her neck around and gazed at the hole in her outstretched wing. "Whoot hoot! So it has." She could see a clean round hole right through her wing. "Just when I thought that wing was getting better, whoot hoot."

"That was a close call. Are you sure you're okay?"

"Looks like I lost a couple of flight feathers, whoot hoot," Chloe said sadly.

"We could have been killed!"

"I always say as long as I am not in the back of an ambulance on my way to the hospital, there's nothing to worry about, whoot hoot!" Chloe said confidently.

Olive wasn't sure what an ambulance was but replied, "I guess that's a good way to look at life. Do you think you'll ever be able to fly again?"

"Luckily, yes, but it's going to take a couple of months for the feathers to grow back so it looks like you are stuck with a lame duck for a while, whoot hoot." Chloe gingerly tested out her wing.

"That's not a problem," Olive said, checking her body for any wounds she may have acquired and finding none. "When we find Santa, I'm sure Grandpapa Nicholas will let you stay at the North Pole if you still need time to recover," Olive said. "Maybe you could even stay with my family in the stable."

"*If* we find him, whoot hoot," Chloe responded, thinking that the prospect was growing ever more doubtful.

"Don't give up hope," Olive cried. "I'm sure we will find him. We have to."

"Well, they say hope springs eternal, whoot hoot."

Not at all sure where they had ended up, Olive looked around and saw that the land was fairly flat dotted with frozen ponds and mounds that looked like out-of-place bumps on such a barren and flat landscape of pure white. "What are those?" she asked, pointing with her nose.

"They are called Pingos, whoot hoot."

"Pingos?"

"Yes, those little hills you are looking at, whoot hoot."

"They look so strange. So where are we?"

"Not sure, but I think they call this place Tuktoyaktuk, whoot hoot," Chloe offered, shaking her head.

"Tuktoyaktuk?" Olive stumbled over the name. "Yikes, that's hard to say."

"Try being an owl, whoot hoot!"

"Do you know which way I should be going? With all that swerving to avoid the bullets I'm sure we've gone off course."

"This is the first time I've ever gone this far north but I think you said you wanted to go west, whoot hoot."

"I've lost all my sense of direction," Olive said with a sigh. "If I had any in the first place. Which way is west?"

"Whoot hoot, now let me put my owl senses on. When I head south, the sun rises on my left and sets on my right..." she muttered. "When I head north, the sun rises on my right and sets on my left."

"And?"

"That's it. That's all I know, whoot hoot."

"What do you mean, that's all you know?" Olive retorted. "I thought you owls were smart?"

"Wise is not the same as smart, whoot hoot. We owls fly north and south. We never go east and west."

"Does the sun set in the west or in the east?"

"The west."

"Well then, which way is west?"

"That-a-way, whoot hoot" Chloe said, hopping around until she faced west.

Olive giggled then headed toward the setting sun.

CHAPTER ELEVEN

Lost

Alabaster and the other elves continued to keep round-the-clock watches of the horizon for any glimpse, sign, or clue of either Santa and the team or Olive's return. They had heard no reports back from Olive and the only reports from all the Santa Helpers in the world said that Santa had visited on Christmas Eve but had not been seen since.

As the New Year approached and with it not even one hopeful sign, Alabaster and the elves decided that the best way they could help right now, to keep their spirits up and their minds off the dire situation, was to get back to work in Santa's Workshop. A whole year may seem far off but when you have to make so many toys, next Christmas feels like it is on you in a heartbeat. So Alabaster handed out assignments, with most elves reporting to the stations they had worked at for many years.

For his part, Alabaster decided to sort some of the mail already floating down the mail chute addressed to Santa thanking him for the wonderful toy or gift the grateful child had received. He wondered why Santa received so many letters asking for gifts but not so many thank-you letters in return. But to Santa, that didn't matter at all. He appreciated every letter he received. It was the giving that was important to him.

"How does Papa Nick handle all this!" he exclaimed as a heap of mail gushed down, burying him in a surge of colourful envelopes and small packages adorned with ribbons, bows, stickers, and drawings of all kinds. Digging himself out, he pushed the new pile off into a corner to make space on Santa's old wooden desk to open each letter and place it in one of the neat piles for Santa to read when he returned. He would never give in to the notion of Santa not returning.

He filed the letters by country of origin, then into age groups from the youngest to the oldest. He knew Santa would read each one attentively, sometimes chuckling at the contents but always appreciating it. He knew some children had barely learned to write and would often have the letters backwards or upside down, but that was fine. Once read, Santa would then mark down the request, check off the Nice List, and then carefully file the letters one-by-one on one of the hundreds of shelves in the file room. He always said, "You never know when you need to help a child who decided to leave Toyland, to remember that he or she too was once a believer."

It was a mystery to Alabaster how the candies, cookies, and other food treats had survived the long trip. Some envelopes leaked from one corner with some kind of unknown sticky syrup. Often he played a game and kept score on a blackboard, as he tried to guess how many of the treats he could identify before opening each envelope.

One small box, flattened in travel, had contained a lemon pudding with whipped cream. He couldn't guess what this one was before he opened it. But when he slit the parcel open, the gooey lemony bits and pieces squirted all over his face and dripped down onto his vest leaving him with his mouth open, speechless.

"Lemon," he muttered, licking the corners of his mouth. "Lemon pudding or pie, I think." A broad smile came over his rosy-cheeked face. He knew that the little boy or girl who had sent it had done so out of love.

The other elves fired up the workshop machinery, started the conveyer belts, opened the paint pots, and clicked on the electronics to start making the toys for next Christmas. Soon, the hustle and bustle of the workshop had cranked up to full speed. The saws buzzed, the lathes spun, and the drills drilled, all making a clamour.

They may not have known the specific request of each child but they did know there were always requests they received every year. Dolls and dollhouses, skates and snowboards, trains and aeroplanes, cars and cuddly teddy bears were always on lists. When it came to computer games and phones, the elves always waited until they had some idea what the new craze would be.

Mrs. Claus gathered her knitting group with some of the older elves and started knitting the scarves, mittens, doll dresses, and sweaters requested every year. All the while, she kept one eye out for her beloved Nicholas. She wouldn't allow hopelessness to cause her to give up. She knew in her heart that they would all come home, and she prayed they would all come home in one piece.

No sooner had Olive taken off toward the west of Tuktoyaktuk than heavy winds began to blow, picking up the fine granules of ice and sending them drifting along the surface of the tundra. Like sand in the desert, the ice crystals stung when they touched skin and got into the eyes of both Olive and Chloe.

"I can't see!" cried Olive as the wind howled louder and stronger.

"I just close my eyes, whoot hoot!" Olive peeped, tucking her head under a wing for protection.

"But then I can't see where I am going," Olive replied, struggling with all her might against the gale. Unable to cover her eyes, Olive ducked her head as best she could and forged on. Soon it was a raging tempest and with each sudden gust Olive was sent tumbling head over heels as Chloe hung on for dear life. Dark storm clouds gathered and snow fell heavily, blinding them as it swirled around like a tornado.

"I wonder if this Blizzard Wizard had anything to do with this or was that story just a superstition," Olive shouted over the howling wind.

"Superstitions are like sunglasses; they make the whole world look dark, whoot hoot!"

"This one could be true," Olive argued.

"Truth is often stretched until it hurts, whoot hoot!"

"Yes, but this truth had a ring of reality."

"Reality and truth are sometimes hard to face, whoot hoot!"

"This truth is blowing really hard right now!" Olive hollered above the deafening storm.

"True! Whoot hoot."

Each time she picked herself up, another blast sent her reeling back and forcing her off course. As each hour passed, Olive was blown this way and that until finally when the wind finally died down she settled deep in a snow bank at the edge of the tree line. All that could be seen of the travellers poking out of the snow was Olive's twitching tail and the tips of her antlers, with a snow-covered Chloe perched on top.

Popping up out the snow bank, Olive shook her head vigorously to clear the clinging snow. Chloe had to grip the antlers with her claws to keep from being flung off.

"Whoot hoot! Am I supposed to hold on for eight seconds?" she screeched as she was whipped around like eggs in a blender.

"Oh, I'm sorry. I forgot you were up there."

"Never saw myself as a rodeo bronco rider, whoot hoot!" she said, her eyes rolling around.

"That was quite the winter storm! I'm still feeling a little dizzy," Olive said struggling to stand. "Are you okay?" Olive felt worn-out and achy from all the tossing and whirling they had done through the storm.

"My whoot hoot lost its whoot, but I'll be okay," Chloe replied, chuckling at her own joke.

"You shouldn't be laughing," Olive said, eyeing the owl. "You could have been really hurt."

"After being hit by a sleigh and having a bullet hole through my wing, this is nothing. Whoot hoot. Anyway laughter is the best shock absorber to ease the blows in life."

Olive gazed around her to get a sense of their strange and alien surroundings. Barely able to keep her eyes open from fatigue, she stared into the dark forest. "It looks a little spooky in there," she said, yawning.

"Fear of the darkness is only fear of the unknown, whoot hoot!"

"I guess so," Olive replied, unconvinced. Three or four sets of eyes stared back at her from the shadows. "In fact, it's more than a little scary."

"Our eyes may play tricks on us but things don't change just because it's dark, whoot hoot!"

Olive's eyes slowly adjusted to the low light beaming from the moon and reflecting off the snow. She leaned forward and strained to see what was behind those eyes of creatures living in the woods. Olive smiled when she realized they were not so sinister after all, but were the eyes of family of pure white arctic hares watching the excitement from the entrance of their warren under the outreaching arm of snow-laden fir tree.

Although curious, the hares trembled, eyeing the strangers that had invaded their comfy home. It wasn't every day they had visitors, especially from strangers. And for rabbits, all strangers made them wary. They never knew when they might have to face a mortal enemy, such as an owl. OWL! As soon as they saw Chloe they all scurried back down into the safety of their burrow never to come out until the coast was clear.

"Well, I guess that's that," Olive said wishing she could have talked to them.

"I get that reaction a lot, whoot hoot!"

"You don't suppose we could entice them back out of the hole, do you? I'd like to ask them where we are."

"I have a feeling that isn't going to happen, whoot hoot."

Olive looked around. "Where do you suppose we are?"

"Not where we were, whoot hoot."

CHAPTER TWELVE
White Storm

Olive's reindeer senses were on high alert making her leery of entering the unknown darkness. She had never been in a forest before. No matter how encouraging Chloe was, her ears and nose twitched uneasily as she tried to make sense of all the unfamiliar smells and sounds. She couldn't shake the sense of foreboding that there was something threatening lurking in the deep shadows. She shuddered at the mere thought of entering the woods.

Although it was a relief to see something other than the endless arctic landscape of snow, ice crystals, and layers and moss-covered rocks, Olive thought it would be difficult and scary to fly through the dark and gloomy woodland. If they travelled in the forest she would never find her way. She decided to skirt the groves of trees in hopes of finding a sign, any sign, of the direction she needed to go. Dodging the forest would allay her uneasy feelings.

They had no idea how far off course they may have flown or if they had been blown south, east, or west during the brutal storm. All they knew was they hadn't travelled north as they would both have recognized the landscape. Knowing that did little to help them find the direction they needed to go now.

"Well, your guess is as good as mine." Olive shrugged her shoulders and looked around.

"It's better to guess with a lot more information, whoot hoot!"

"No kidding! So what's your best guess?"

"I'm never good at second guessing, whoot hoot!"

"You said before that when you fly north, the sun sets on your left, when you fly south, the sun sets on your right," Olive reminded her companion. "So if we face the way the sun sets we are heading west, yes?"

"Whoot hoot! Eureka!"

"That was easy!" Olive said, feeling quite proud of herself. "We'll be on our way in no time!"

"But…"

"But what?"

"It's cloudy, whoot hoot," Chloe said sadly.

"Good point. Now what?"

"Eeny, meany, miny mo? Whoot hoot!"

"I can't just guess, Chloe."

"Whoot hoot, you know what they say, 'A reindeer going nowhere will surely never find her destination.'"

"I know, I'll fly up high and see which way we need to go," Olive said, excited by her new idea.

"Whoot hoot, let's go!"

Olive jumped up expecting to fly as usual only wobble unsteadily before floating back to the ground. "Oh, oh," Olive gasped. Had her magic dust been completely drained while she fought the winter storm? "I think I need to rest for awhile."

"Whoot hoot! What's up?"

"I can't fly right now. I guess the storm took a lot of my energy and now I need to rest so my magic dust can renew itself."

In the distance a long bone-shivering howl echoed through the tree branches. Suddenly, all life went instantly silent, as still as gravestones.

"What was that?" Olive shivered. She had never heard such a hair-raising sound. Resting was out of the question now.

"I hope it's not what I think it is, whoot hoot,"

"And that is…?"

"White Storm, whoot hooooot!"

"Is that the wolf Sly was talking about?"

"Whoot hoot, yeah, and he has a wolf pack of savage beasts they call the Howling Dozen. They are a pretty tough gang in these parts." Chloe knew they might be in a little trouble. "I don't want to die, I don't want to die, whoot hoot," Chloe squawked, almost dancing with a fear.

"Maybe he can help us find our way?" Olive said, thinking she could make friends with them.

"I really don't think so, whoot hoot," Chloe protested. "I have seen wolf packs hunt before but only from the safety of a high perch in a tall Douglas fir."

"Wolves are just dogs…aren't they?" Olive guessed. "Aren't they supposed to be man's best friend?"

"Whoot hoot! One way to put it, I guess." Chloe rolled her eyes. "But I've never seen them being friends with a reindeer."

"But…"

"Wolves are wild and not like your friendly down-home poodle. These guys are mean, meaner, and meanest! Whoot hoot."

"They can't be that bad, can they?"

"Wolves are always hungry, always hunting for their next meal and would tear any reindeer, caribou, or elk limb from limb if they get the chance, whoot hoot," she said beginning to dance again.

"Maybe they are…"

"And they especially like reindeer, whoot hoot!"

Realizing Chloe was quite serious Olive gulped as fear washed over her. She went pale, and when she heard another long, creepy howl vibrate from the deep forest she shuddered. This time, the haunting sound was even closer.

"I think we should be going…quickly," Olive said, now fearing the worst.

"Whoot hoot, whoot hoot, good idea," Chloe gasped. Forgetting that her damaged wing would not work properly, she instinctively flapped her wings frantically but stayed rooted to Olive's antlers.

Olive tried to run away from the baying wolves but the snowdrift was so deep she found herself buried up to her chest. It was far too deep to wade through. "Wow! We're not going too far ploughing through this," Olive panted, backing her way out.

"Whoot hoot the snow is a lot deeper out in the open. Maybe we should go through the forest?"

"But, but…what about the wolves?"

"Whoot hoot. Run, run you must."

"Well, here goes." Olive still felt weak, and as she entered the woods she stayed close to its edge, not making a sound. But the farther she went, the deeper into the shadows the paths led, and the more eerie the towering trees felt.

"What was that?" Olive jumped at the sharp crack of a branch off to her right and her head snapped around. But she saw nothing.

It felt like hungry eyes watched her from all directions and more strange noises caused her to jump this way then that to catch a glimpse of whatever or whoever was there. *Are my eyes and ears tricking me?* Olive wondered. *Am I being superstitious?* Shadows created more shadows, and the cold breeze through the branches made the trees crack and groan.

Chloe's head swivelled constantly first to the left, then right and, as only owls can do, all the way around to the back but she saw nothing either. Looking down she squealed, "Whoot hoot, tracks in snow, tracks in snow."

"Olive saw the big paw prints too. "There are so many all heading all the same way, what do you think made them?"

"Whoot hoot, not lemmings, nor bunnies."

"Too small for reindeer or humans," Olive said as she inspected the prints. "Recent too. Made after the storm."

"Wolves, whoot hoot, wolves, must be wolves."

"You might be right Chloe. I think we'll head the other way. We're lost anyway but there's no point in walking straight into a pack of wolves."

"Whoot hoot, the jaws of death?"

"That's one way of putting it."

With Chloe riding atop her antlers, Olive turned and dashed in another direction. As she darted and leapt over fallen logs along the pathway, and dodged rocks and bushes, the track got darker and narrower until branches brushed her flanks. She had the unsettling feeling they were being led down a path but not knowing any better, carried on anyway.

Natural survival instinct drove her on, away from the footprints that meant danger. Her suspicions grew more insistent and when they turned a corner she realized her fears were real.

"Whoa!" Olive screamed planting her feet firmly on the ground just before running straight into the trap.

"Well, what do we have here?" growled the white wolf with his head lowered. He stood on top of a rock with his gnarly, shaggy-haired pack surrounding him in the shadows. All eyes leered at the delicious prey they had snared in their carefully planned trap.

"Your plan worked, White Storm," said a grey wolf.

"Of course it worked, fool! I am the master of deception."

"Of course, Your Highness-ness. I was just…"

"Shut-up, fool. Now let us snag our dinner." White Storm leapt off the rock and with his long lean body he lunged toward Olive.

"Ruuuuuuuuuuuun! Whoot hoot, whoot hoot, whoot hoot! Ruuuuuuuuuun!" Chloe shrieked.

Olive leapt sideways to avoid White Storm's lunge, bowled over a black wolf, and ran as fast as her hooves would carry her. She bolted through the trees darting one way then the other with the wolves in hot pursuit, gaining ground as they ran. Two wolves flanked her on each side keeping her corralled while White Storm led the rest to close in behind her. She only had one way to go and that was straight ahead.

Terror ripped through Olive's body. Her heart raced as she darted this way and that do dodge the snapping fangs of the flanking wolves. This was all part of White Storm's plan.

He knew that a deer's natural instinct was to panic once singled out and no longer within the safety of her herd.

"We'll have her soon, boys. It's just a matter of time," White Storm said, confidently loping in chase.

Olive saw a clearing up ahead and ran straight for it. "We've only got one chance, I hope this works," she whispered to Chloe.

"Whoot hoot, whatever it is, we need a miracle right now!" Chloe screeched just as White Storm snapped at Olive's heels. "I mean right now! Whoot hoot!"

Olive broke into the clearing and jumped for her life, praying she had enough re-energized magic dust to allow her fly. Her heels left the ground and she flew upward at the same moment the wolves pounced to take down their prey. Once committed, the wolves couldn't stop, and one by one they plowed into the deep snow banks that Olive had known where there. As they fell, each one landed on top of a furious White Storm who was buried beneath the heap.

"Get off me, you fools!" snarled the wolf pack leader trying to dig out from under the pile of his twelve entangled followers. "After her, you dogs! After her!" he screamed.

The fading magic kept Olive and her passenger just off the ground, allowing her to fly farther into the gap. She could feel the magic draining from her but she knew she had to use every last drop to get as far away as possible from the menacing, savage pack. Out here in the open she could see them coming and if need be, she could make another mad dash for safety.

She was exhausted when her magic energy finally ran out causing her to land heavily to the sound of a loud cracking noise underneath her. She looked around and was relieved to see no wolves.

"That was a close call," she said. She knew it wouldn't be long before they would be once again upon her.

"Whoot hoot, we're not out of the woods yet. Whoot hoot."

Olive looked around at the vast open space where they were.

"Whoot hoot, you know what I mean."

Olive knew what Chloe meant but more cracking noises beneath her caused her to look down. She scraped the surface to clear the snow and saw the tell tale layer of ice and knew she was standing on a snow covered lake. "Oh, oh." They had escaped one peril only to be threatened by another.

"Whoot hoot, see what I mean? Out of the pot and into the fire, they say."

"We need to get off this ice as soon as we can," Olive said, scampering toward the other side of the lake. At each step the ice cracked but she had lived all her life on ice so she knew how to tread lightly and spread her weight.

As she made her way gingerly across the surface, one well-placed step at a time, she once again heard the haunting howl of wolves. "Don't they ever give up?" she cried in despair.

"Whoot hoot, not when supper is served."

"I really didn't find that funny, Chloe." She looked back and saw that White Storm had broken free of the snow bank and was now leading the charge across the ice.

Chloe could see the wolves slipping and sliding, getting no traction on the ice. "Whoot hoot, those wolves should be wary."

"What do you mean, Chloe?"

"Before following a leader, it is wise to see where he is leading them, whoot hoot."

The rest of the pack hesitated as their feet skidded in all directions. Paws splayed out as they fell flat on their faces.

At the moment Chloe finished saying her wise words, the ice broke and one after another each of the ravenous pack of wolves fell into the freezing water.

Panic now filled the wolves' eyes at the shock of the icy water and their poor swimming skills. "See how that feels," shouted a triumphant Olive.

In their terror, they seemed to forget all about chasing Olive and now thrashed about trying to reach solid ground. White Storm, however, wasn't giving up and tried with all his might to pursue Olive but every time his paws reached solid ice, it broke off sending him back into the icy water. Onward he went, moving ever deeper into the middle of the lake. His attack instinct drove him on, unaware to the impending danger.

The wolves on the shore howled at him to turn back.

"I won't let our victim escape!" he bayed. With his might, he plunged on through the numbing water. Each paddle grew slower and weaker than the last, and it looked to Olive like he might end his by drowning. He growled and leered at his escaping prey then reluctantly turned back, following the rest of his scrambling pack.

One by one, they swam toward the safety of land where they had come from. Olive could see them shivering and shaking their fur coats to get the quickly forming ice off before they froze to death.

The last to reach the shore was White Storm who furiously shook his fur then turned back to see Olive and

Chloe on safely on the other side. "We will meet another day, I promise you that! You won't escape me next time," he howled. Then he turned and skulked back into the woods.

The other wolves followed. They hadn't brought down their evening meal and their bellies would go hungry again tonight. They would also have to face White Storm's terrible wrath.

Olive continued to watch them until she saw each wolf disappear into the dark shadows of the woods.

"Let's get out of here," she said.

"Defeat never comes to a wolf until he admits it, whoot hoot!"

"I have a feeling he hasn't admitted it yet. Not by a long shot."

CHAPTER THIRTEEN
Bruce the Christmoose

Wearily, Olive staggered up the lake's snow-covered bank and through thinly wooded rocky ground at the lake edge. Her right leg throbbed, causing her to limp. "If all I got out of that was a sore leg, I consider us lucky," Olive muttered, wincing as she plodded on.

"Whoot hoot. Good luck often has the odor of perspiration about it," Chloe said seeing that Olive was still sweating from her frantic run.

"You got that right Chloe. I know I have to rest but I want to put some space between White Storm and his minions."

She still had no idea where she was or where she was going but knew she couldn't stay where they were. A limping animal doesn't have a chance in the wilderness if another predator were to find them. If it weren't the wolves, it could be a black bear, or a mountain lion picking up her scent. She knew she had to find shelter and soon.

Olive and Chloe hobbled silently along for the rest of the day, moving in what they thought was a westerly direction. Olive's ears and nosed twitched, scanning all around. "Do you see any sign of the wolves, Chloe?"

"Whoot hoot, not a sign, not a sound, not a scent."

Olive breathed a small sigh of relief when they reached the lowlands of some mountains and could see the craggy peaks up ahead. At least there they should be able to find some cover and hide for a while.

By the time they decided to look for a place to rest, Olive's limp had grown worse. Her knee had swollen to the point where she could hardly put any weight on it. As the sun edged over the horizon and the evening's cold air settled in, Olive was so tired she was nodding off to sleep as she walked. She had begun wandering off the path, and when her hoof stumbled or she broke a branch, she startled awake before returning to her hazy, fumbling walk. She knew she couldn't go on much longer.

"Whoot hoot, I saw something move," Chloe whispered.

"Huh, where?" Olive snapped awake.

"Whoot hoot, up ahead."

Olive stared into the half-light and saw a shadow coming toward them. "Oh great! Not more wolves!"

Olive knew there was no way she could outrun them so she looked for a place to make her last stand and backed up to a large rock. She thought she could defend herself using her antlers and front hooves like she did playing games in the reindeer yard. She was thankful that she had practiced this many times with the other reindeer in play. This time, though, it was for real. She prepared herself for a life and death struggle. "Okay busters, come and feel the points of my antlers."

The sound of heavy hoof clomps and grunting snorts coming from within the trees grew louder and closer. "That animal sounds awfully big," she whispered, staring intently into the gloom. "I didn't know wolves grew that big." She heard another tree branch break but still saw nothing, nothing at all. All she heard was the slight breeze coming from the wrong direction rustling the branches, and the steady sound of foot falls.

"Whoot hoot, that's one big, big gigantic wolf!"

"Shhhh, it may not have seen us. Keep as still and quiet as you can." Olive hushed Chloe and sniffed the air, but the snow-covered branches blocked her view and there was nothing on the wind. "Do you see anything?" she whispered knowing an owl's eyesight was better than hers.

Chloe's sharp eyes were focused on seeing anything that moved but she saw nothing other than snow falling off a nearby branch. "Whoot hoot, nothing," she reported in a whisper.

The moments passed like thick syrup from a bottle, and the silence made Olive so nervous she began to back up, as slowly and quietly as she could to put some distance between whatever beast was stalking her and their last defence. Then she hit something solid.

"Do you mind? Ye're stepping on my hoof," boomed voice with a Scottish accent from behind them. The creature yanked its hoof out from under Olive's.

"Whaaat?" Olive spun toward the thunderous sound, preparing to defend herself against whatever it was.

"Ye'd be in big trouble if I were a Sasquatch," the deep voice said. "He woulda scrambled yer brains by now."

"Whoa, you, you, you're a moose!" Olive cried out. "I mean a really, really big moose." She craned her neck up to look at him. In front of her was an immense moose, with antlers wider than the back of Santa's sleigh, and decorated with Christmas ornaments, strings of tinsel, and coloured glass balls.

"Yup, that'd be me, Bruce the Moose," he said rolling the 'r'. "And now young lassie, my foot hurts."

"I'm so sorry," Olive apologized. "We thought you were wolves."

"They're behind you a wee ways back."

"They are?" Olive gasped, spinning in every direction.

"Ye won't see those varmints so easily. Their stock in trade is sneaking up on unsuspecting deeries like you," Bruce explained calmly, his Christmas decorations jingling. "With all that noise ye were makin' they would have had ye by now."

"Aren't you worried about them?"

"Och, look at me lass. They aren't no fools. I'd kick 'em into next week if they ever wanted a piece of me and they know it."

"How did they know where we were going?"

"Whoot hoot, no matter what you do, someone always knew you would," Chloe chirped.

"The owl is right. You can fool them once but rarely twice, or you make fools of them," Bruce said.

"Whoot hoot, fool me once, shame on you. Fool me twice, shame on me."

"Okay, okay, I get it," Olive said. "I see you're dressed festively." Olive observed the Christmas decorations strewn over Bruce's antlers.

"It's that time of year and I love Christmas," Bruce replied cheerfully.

"I do too but now we need a place to hide for a while. I hope our luck doesn't run out."

"Whoot hoot, luck always runs out for someone who's depending on it."

"I know a cave not too far from here. I use it sometimes to get out of the bad weather," Bruce offered.

"Oh, that would be wonderful," Olive said. She stepped forward, favouring her swollen right leg. "I really need a place to rest for a while."

"I see ye've been hurt. I'll come with ye and show the way and perhaps keep those mangy mutts at bay if need be."

"Oh, Bruce, I can't thank you enough for sharing your cave."

"Och, it's not my cave lassy, it's Mizzy's."

"Mizzy's?"

"Yes, Mizz the Grizz. It's hers when she goes into her big sleep for the winter."

"You mean a grizzly bear?" Olive's mouth fell open.

"Och, aye, but she's sound asleep for another three months," Bruce added casually. "Ye can stay as long as ye don't mind her snoring. She can get a wee bit loud now and then."

"But, but what if she wakes up?"

"I don't know, she's never done that whenever I've taken leave to use it for a wee while," Bruce answered confidently. "Now lean on me and I'll help ye up the hill."

They made their way up a narrowing path that switched back a couple of times and almost disappeared altogether when suddenly, they came upon the cave entrance. The way into the cave was narrow and well hidden but Olive knew their tracks in the snow leading up to it would be a telltale sign for White Storm to follow. Still, she had to take the chance if she was ever wanted to fly again.

"Well, here goes," Olive said. "Nothing ventured, nothing gained." She slipped through the slender opening.

"Whoot hoot, copying is the best form of flattery."

Olive rolled her eyes. She was beginning to sound just like Chloe. Once inside, the passageway wound its way around ending at a large opening not too far in. Dim light filtered in from a small hole above showing Olive three separate passageways breaking off from this one and leading deeper into the cave. They all could hear the throaty snoring rumbling from deep in the darkness beyond but they couldn't tell from which passage it came. It seemed to echo from all of them all at once. "You weren't kidding about the snoring, were you?" Olive said. It reverberated off the walls.

"Think of it as kind of a friend, lassie."

"Why is that, Bruce?"

"Because if it ever stops, you'll know to run!"

"Good point," Olive replied, feeling a little more comfortable. She settled down to rest. Chloe hopped off her antler perch and snuggled in between Olive's forelegs. Escaping the wolves had been an ordeal for her too and she needed sleep as well.

"Your owl seems quite friendly," Bruce commented.

"She was hurt flying into Santa's sleigh so I'm giving her a lift until her wing mends. It didn't help that she got shot too."

"Whoot hoot, he doesn't need to know everything," Chloe muttered. She was still a little embarrassed about flying into Santa's sleigh.

"Oh, I'm sure Bruce won't tell anyone. There's no shame in accepting a little help from your friends now and then."

"Whoot hoot, I've never had one before."

"What's that, Chloe?"

"A friend, whoot hoot."

Olive smiled and gently nuzzled her friend. "Well, you have one now."

Bruce positioned himself between Olive and the cave entrance in case the wolves became confident enough to enter a sleeping grizzly's den. "Santa's sleigh? I really like Santa," he said fondly giving his decorations a little shake.

"I could hardly tell," Olive said, grinning as she surveyed Bruce's decorations. "I like Santa as well." She didn't want to say much more as she remembered what Grandmama Claus had warned her about telling strangers who she was.

"Tell me, lass, what brings ye out here in the wilderness? Ye don't belong here, that'll be sure."

"Is it that obvious?" Olive asked. She felt a little embarrassed that it was so noticeable that she wasn't worldly-wise.

"Whoot hoot, your turn," Chloe said with a smirk.

"Well, I'm not from here. I'm from up north and not used to wolves…or mooses."

"How far up north do you mean?" Bruce asked, tilting his head. "There's not much 'up north' except for polar bears and foxes."

"There are muskoxen," Olive replied.

"I believe the only reindeer that far north are Santa's reindeer," Bruce claimed, giving Olive a prickly stare.

"Okay, you got me. I am Olive, daughter of Prancer and a reindeer in training to perhaps one day fly with Santa on his trip every Christmas Eve," she said.

"Can't you fly?"

"I can but I haven't had the chance to rest. When my magic dust runs low I need to regenerate it. Yesterday, we got caught in a storm and we had to fight it all through the night, which exhausted me completely," she said with a sigh, "and when I tried to get the rest I needed, White Storm and his dirty Howling Dozen showed up and tried to catch us for dinner."

"And how did ye hurt yer leg, lassie?"

"I hurt my leg landing hard on an ice lake while fleeing from the wolves."

"So you *are* one of Santa's reindeer! Just as I suspected!" Bruce told her with an air of satisfaction. "So what brings you all the way out here, lassie?"

"Grandmama Claus sent me out to find Santa after he didn't return home from his Christmas Eve trip."

"Aha! That's why I heard from Alabaster!"

Olive gaped at the moose. "You know Alabaster?"

"Ooops," Bruce bit his lip. It was too late to swallow the words now. "It looks like I've got some 'fessing up to do as well. I am in training to become one of Santa's Helpers. I'm not supposed to tell anyone but...but it just sneaked out."

"A Santa's Helper! That's awesome!"

"My real name is Bruce the Christmoose and I watch all the children in the area and report back if they've been good or bad throughout the year."

"Wow! I never would have thought a moose could be a Santa's Helper."

"Och, ye just never know who may be a Santa's Helper. They're not just shopping mall elves and Santas, you know. Over the many years, Santa has got to know and become friends with many who believe in his love. It could be a crow, a dog, a neighbour, or a stranger. That's the whole point—you just never know."

112

"Someone can't help everyone but everyone can help someone, whoot hoot!" Chloe mumbled, half asleep and snuggled up against Olive's warm belly.

"The kids never notice me. I just watch from a distance, say nothing, and just observe. I report any one being mean or nasty especially when they're out of sight from their parents' eyes."

"Wow, I thought kids were always good. I never thought they might be bad," Olive said, surprised.

"Och, children can be little devils, you know, if they don't mind their manners. When caught, they'll always try to make excuses."

"Whoot hoot, excuses are usually a thin skin of falsehood stretched over a bald-faced lie."

"That's a bit harsh, Chloe," Olive observed. She looked up at Bruce again. "So what else do you do?"

"I did help one time with a gift for a child that Santa missed because she had moved. She had no idea it was me who reached through the window and put the present under her tree."

"That is so good of you!" Olive declared. "But what have you heard from Alabaster?"

"A message went out over Santa's hotline a few days ago asking if we had seen Santa and his famous reindeer team. Later on, they called again asking if I had seen you but at that time, I hadn't seen you, either. I'll be sure to let them know in the morning that you are a little worse for wear but doing just fine."

"Thank-you, Bruce. I know Grandmama will be happy to hear from you."

"Ye're welcome, lass. It's always good to be on the good side of Grandmama." Bruce's brow twisted into a frown. "Do you know what happened to Santa?"

"No. Grandmama Claus hopes he may be somewhere in Alaska. We just hope he's not hurt or, or…" The lump in Olive's throat prevented the words from getting out.

"I understand lassie, but if I know Santa, he'll be fine. I just hope he hasn't got mixed up with the Blizzard Wizard."

"You're the second person who has mentioned the Blizzard Wizard."

"Och he's a very bad wizard indeed! He's the one responsible for the storm you went through last night, lassie. I'm sure of it."

"Why is he so mean?"

"They say he was a sea captain who was trying to find his way through the Northwest Passage when the ship froze up in the ice. He and his crew all died on Christmas Day and since then he's never liked Christmas."

"What? Someone who doesn't like Christmas!"

"I don't get it either, lass," Bruce said, shaking his head sadly.

"He had better not have done anything to my Grandpapa Nick," Olive declared, "or he'll feel the points of my antlers!"

"Before you go takin' on the world, little one, ye're gonna have to get a wee bit o' rest and get a fresh start in the morning."

"I guess you're right," Olive said. She tucked her head down against Chloe's feathers.

Bruce the Christmoose stood guard at the entrance to the cave while his new friends soundly dozed.

As the sun glanced into the cave in the early morning, Olive's dreams were abruptly interrupted by crashing, clanking, yelping, and growling. "What was that?" she cried, blinking and shaking awake.

"You'd better run, lass. The mangy wolves have found ye," Bruce bellowed as he rammed another attacker out of the cave.

"Oh my!" Olive said, leaping to her feet, now wide-awake.

"Let me at her," screamed White Storm trying to pass Bruce's massive antlers. "No one makes a fool out of me and gets away with it," he howled.

"Not if I have anything to say about it, laddie," Bruce grunted, easily tossing White Storm back through the cave entrance.

The wolf yelped as he landed hard on the rocks.

"HE BUSTED MY BALLS!" Bruce bawled, seeing his broken decorations scattered about the cave floor. "That varmint BUSTED MY BALLS!"

"Your balls? Oh dear, how can I help?" inquired Olive, biting the inside of her cheek to keep from laughing out loud. She had never seen a moose go into a rage before but she was sure glad that it was the wolves he was taking it out on and not her. Furry bodies flew off in every direction.

"Touch my balls, will ye? I do not think so," Bruce hollered yelled tossing another wolf out the door.

"Whoot hoot, he really likes his decorations, doesn't he?"

"There's nothing you can do here, lass. Ye're gonna have to get yerself out of here before there's too many for me to handle."

"But what about you?"

"Do not worry about me, lass. You need to go find Grandpapa Nicholas. I'll be okay, don't you worry about that!"

"But…"

"No buts, young lady. Get yourself gone."

"You too, my highland laddie, and take your balls with you!" growled a grumpy voice behind her.

Olive spun around. She gasped, and her eyes nearly popped out of their sockets. "Mizz…the Grizz!" she stammered.

Towering up on her massive hind legs was the den's owner, the grizzly bear, and she was *not* in a good mood. The bear roared the most piercing, furious bellow letting all within hearing distance know that she was not happy about being awakened from her winter hibernation.

With a squeal, Chloe leapt onto Olive's shoulders, gripping hard with her claws. Then Olive sprang straight up and found herself in mid-air. At the sight of the grizzly, the wolves scattered as fast as their paws could carry them, followed by an anxious Bruce the Christmoose, trailing his decorations behind him.

Every one of them scrambled for the caves entrance, fleeing from Mizz the Grizz. Olive knew that there was is nothing worse than enraging a grizzly bear while in hibernation, especially if she has cubs to protect.

Mizz the Grizz stood between Olive and the cave entrance snorting and grunting after the departing trespassers and making sure no one came back. Now, Mizz the Grizz blocked Olive's exit and there was no way around her. Olive cast about her for another exit and saw the circle of light above her. Somehow she had to get out through the narrow hole in the ceiling of the cave.

"Hang on," she said to Chloe.

At the sound of Olive's voice, Mizz the Grizz whirled around, no longer in the mood to be gracious. She gave a mighty roar and lunged toward Olive.

Olive sprinted upward with Chloe clinging desperately to her back, just in time to miss the swipe of Mizz's gigantic paw with its enormous claws. Olive remembered Agalu's claws and had no desire to feel Mizz's. She hovered near the top of the cave while the irritated bear lunged at her again and again.

"Chloe, you go out first." Olive could feel Mizz's hot breath with each infuriated roar. Chloe hopped out through the narrow hole first followed by Olive, who squeezed through the small opening into the fresh air. The crotchety old bear thundered at her a few more times, until her roar became a rumble.

From below on the rocks, Bruce called out, "Safe journey, little one."

Olive gave a shake and looked around. Not one cowardly wolf was anywhere to be seen. She hoped she would never have to see them ever again. "Thank you, Bruce, for all your help. I'll be sure to tell Santa of all you've done for us," Olive promised.

"I would appreciate that, lassie."

"I wouldn't have survived the wolves if it hadn't beenfor you," she said sincerely.

"No problem there, lass, I was glad to help," Bruce said flicking a tinsel garland back up into place.

"What do you plan to do now?" Olive asked.

"I'm going to have a wee bit of fun and find some doggies' behinds to kick."

"Well, we're off to find Santa and my papa."

"And which way would that be, lassie?"

"I'm heading for Alaska."

"That would be west from here, lassie,"

"Thank you, er…which way is west?"

"You need to go that-a-way," Bruce tilted his huge antlers untidily adorned with tinsel and broken ornaments.

"Oh…right. And good luck getting your balls back," Olive said, stifling a giggle.

"No worries, little one. I'll have them back in no time," Bruce answered. He gave Olive a quizzical look then simply shrugged.

Chloe hopped up on Olive's antlers and the pair took off. Bruce slowly grew smaller and smaller as Olive kicked her refreshed legs and headed upward and westward. "We have sure met some nice folks out here," Olive said, thinking of Sly and Bruce.

Chloe thought about their close calls with the human hunters, the wolves, and Mizz the Grizz. "And some not so nice ones, whoot hoot."

CHAPTER FOURTEEN
Rusty and Dusty

Olive felt so much better now and was relieved that she could stretch her legs and fly once again. With the swelling all but gone, her sore leg felt healthy and strong after her good night's sleep, even if they did have a rude awakening.

"Mizz the Grizz sure woke up grouchy, didn't she?" Olive commented, thinking back to the events earlier that morning.

"A grouch thinks the world is against them…and generally it is! Whoot hoot!"

"Of course, we did disturb her winter sleep like a clanging alarm clock."

"Whoot hoot, the trouble with alarm clocks is that they always go off when you're asleep," Chloe said, chuckling at her own wit.

"I hope she doesn't have any problems getting back to sleep," she mused. "I see how grumpy she is when she doesn't get a long enough rest."

"Whoot hoot, if she is like me I always need thirty minutes more. But she might need another month!"

As they cruised along over trees, patches of snow, hills and valleys, Olive began to think again about the problem at hand. She hoped Grandmama Claus picked the right reindeer for this mission because it bothered her that she still has no idea where Santa and the team could be. *Perhaps Rollo would have been a better pick, after all*, she thought, filling with self-doubt.

"Whoot hoot, a penny for your thoughts," Chloe said, peering into Olive's face.

"I'm just thinking about Santa, my Papa, and the rest of the team. I'm getting worried. We still have no idea where they might be. If it was just a matter of his sleigh crash landing, surely somebody would have seen it and reported it back to the North Pole by now."

"Whoot hoot, what else?"

"First, nobody has seen any trace or heard of them, correct?"

"Whoot hoot, correct."

"Second, not even Bruce the Christmoose, has heard anything over the Santa Hotline of any reindeer making their way back home, and he's a Santa Helper in training!"

"Whoot hoot, true."

"And third, everybody keeps talking about this Blizzard Wizard and I'm wondering if he has had anything to do with this."

"Whoot hoot, to feed his fire for revenge, he wants the ice storms that hurt him to hurt everyone else but in the end, he will always left out in the cold."

"I have learned that humans can be cruel," she said with a sigh.

A strange yelping sound coming from below interrupted Olive's thoughts. 'Did you hear that?"

"Whoot hoot, sounds like more trouble…for us."

As they crested a snowy hill, she saw two large dogs jumping up and down and pulling on something. They were attached to it and unable to free themselves.

"More wolves?" Olive guessed. "What do you think Chloe?"

"Whoot hoot, I don't think they are wolves," Chloe whispered.

"What makes you say that? They look like some kind of wolf."

"Whoot hoot, their tails are wagging like they are happy to see us."

Olive could see that indeed the dogs looked happy to see them and were different from White Storm and the shaggy wolves that ran with him. As she got closer she could see that the dogs were in harnesses connected to an overturned dog sled. "I think we need to see if they need our help."

"Whoot hoot, what could it hurt?" Chloe snorted. "I don't see any killer whales, or wolves, or grizzly bears around."

Olive swooped down and landed near the excited dogs who lunged and yanked at their harnesses. "Are you guys okay?" she asked.

"Yup, yup, yup we crashed, we crashed, we crashed," said the grey one.

"Uh huh, uh huh, chased by wolves we were, chased, chased, chased," said the red-tinged one.

"Whoot hoot, here we go again," Chloe groaned.

"We have had our fair share of White Storm and his mangy Howling Dozen. They don't give up easily do they?" Olive said.

"Yup, yup, yup. We ran, ran, ran," replied the grey dog.

"Uh huh, uh huh, chased by wolves we were, we were," said the red-tinged one again.

"A little simple, aren't they," Chloe noted. "But I guess you don't have to have much education to pull a sled, whoot hoot."

"Hey! My papa pulls a sleigh, and one day I want to pull one, too!" Olive countered.

Chloe gulped. "But you guys pull a sleigh not a dog sled," she amended quickly. "Santa's sleigh, in fact. Big difference, BIG, BIG difference, whoot hoot." She drew her good wing across her brow.

Ignoring Chloe, Olive said, "Let me see if I can get you unstuck." One of the sled runners had wedged between two rocks buried under the snow. Not really knowing how dog sleds were built, she didn't see any other damage. Canvas covered whatever was in the sled and there didn't seem to be a humankind driver around.

"Let me see if I can pull you back," Olive grabbed the drive handle and pulled with all her might but the sled was wedged in tight. She tried again, with no success. "Hmm, this is going to be more difficult than I thought."

"Yup, yup, yup, stuck, stuck, stuck," the grey dog yapped.

"Uh huh, uh huh, we are stuck, stuck, stuck," repeated the other one.

"Whoot hoot, they must make their parents proud," Chloe said, shaking her head. "They say it is impossible to make wisdom hereditary."

"Oh stop it, Chloe, they can't help it. They are…uh, what are you guys?"

"I'm Dusty the Husky," said the grey one.

"I'm Rusty the Husky," said the red tinged one.

"Whoot hoot, that figures," Chloe said, rolling her eyes.

"Where is the rest of the dog team," Olive asked noticing two empty harnesses.

"Yup, yup, yup, ran away, ran away, ran away," said Dusty.

"Uh huh, uh huh, ran, ran, ran," said Rusty.

Just then the air was pierced by a sound that sliced terror into Olive's heart once again. The blood curdling, evil howl sent a shiver of fear up and down her spine.

"Awoooooooh!"

"Oh no! Not again!" She looked up to the sky. "If it isn't for bad luck, we wouldn't have any luck at all."

White Storm and his Howling Dozen had caught up to the dog sled team that had bolted for their lives the first time they came upon them. This time he did not see the humankind child with the stick that makes loud noises and kills his brothers.

"This should be easy," White Storm snarled under his breath from the shadows of the forest.

Hidden from sight, the Howling Dozen slunk through the woods and positioned themselves for the planned attack.

"No humankind in sight," said the alpha female. Even if there was a boy child, all wolves were leery of humankind because they kill her kind not for food but out of fear. "It looks like those dumb mutts got themselves stuck."

"And only two."

"Couldn't be easier," she said, drooling.

Then White Storm noticed Olive, "And what do we have here? Our little rat that got away as well! This keeps getting any better!"

"Yessssss!" slobbered a few others at the prospect of a meal.

"And no big ol' moose to protect them!" said the alpha female. "I still have the bruises from when he flung me."

"What could be better, boys? Lunch and dinner all at once!" White Storm cried with glee, then shouted, "After them!"

At once, Olive saw the wolves racing out of their hiding places in the woods, attacking from all directions. They were fast and closing swiftly across the open countryside. Panic rushed through her. There was nowhere to run, "What do we do?" she cried, dancing about.

"There's nowhere to go but up, whoot hoot!"

"But I can't just leave them," she cried, seeing the fear in the big eyes of Rusty and Dusty, begging for help. She knew there was no way out for them unless she could do something.

"I have an idea," she said.

"That's what I'm afraid of, whoot hoot!"

Olive slid her head into one of the empty harnesses and sprang up into the air, lifting the huskies off the ground. Kicking her legs and pulling with all her strength, she tugged on the reins as hard as she could. The straps bit into her chest as she strained to heave upward, struggling to free the sled. Even Chloe flapped her good wing to get more lift. She could see the wolves almost upon them.

"Whoot hoot, puuuuuuullllllll!" she screeched.

Rusty and Dusty ran in mid-air as if to help but only floated helplessly just above the ground. Olive bore down with energy that came from somewhere deep within her and heaved once more with all her might.

The first wolf to reach them leapt up, snapping at Dusty's back leg, when just then the sled snapped loose from the rocky crag and sprang into the air. The wolf's jaws bit into thin air when Dusty suddenly lurched out of reach. Two wolves fell hard off the back of the sled sending them yelping and limping back toward the rest of the pack as the sled hung in mid air, out of reach.

"Not again!" White Storm snarled, as he took a running leap and snagged one of the sled runners but even he could not hold on for long and plunged back into the snow.

Olive smiled as she rose higher and could see the wolves circling the gap they had vacated. Those wolves would not be getting her or the huskies today…as long as her magic held out.

"Which way should we go?"

"Yup, yup, yup. Village, village, village," yipped Dusty.

"Uh huh, uh huh, fly, fly, fly," yapped Rusty.

"Which way is that?"

"Yup, yup, yup that-a-way, that-a-way, that-a-way," Dusty replied, pointing with her paw.

"Uh huh, uh huh, that-a-way," said Rusty agreed, pointing too.

Meanwhile below, the alpha female wolf sneered at White Storm. "Are you going to let them get away for a third time?"

"Never!" He turned to the pack. "After them!"

Olive whizzed along as fast as she would allow herself toward the village the huskies had pointed to hoping they could outdistance the wolves. She knew the wolves were just as determined as she, and White Storm led the pack in pursuit. They weren't far behind. How long could the wolves keep up the pace running through the snow before they exhausted themselves, she wondered. But she did not know these predators' determination when chasing a kill.

"Whoot hoot, they won't give up, if that's what you're thinking, Olive. They'll never give up."

Olive desperately hoped her magic dust would last long enough to make it to safety. "I just pray we can make it to the village in time."

"Life is fragile, handle it with prayer, whoot hoot!"

"Then you'd better get praying," Olive panted.

Weaving in and out of trees to keep low and conserve her magic, Olive made her way through the wilderness. The huskies yelped whenever the sled brushed treetops or snagged a branch, and with only a few close calls, Olive was becoming quite nimble and skilled at pulling a sled as she laced her way through the trees.

"Whoot hoot, your Grandpapa Nicholas and your papa would be so proud of you right now."

"What do you mean, Chloe?" Olive strained at the weight dragging behind her.

"You're pulling your own sleigh just like your papa and his brothers do every Christmas time, whoot hoot!"

In all the excitement, Olive hadn't noticed what she was actually achieving. Any other time she would have been pleased with herself. Pulling a sleigh would have been considered one of her greatest achievements even if this were just a dog sled, so much smaller and lighter than Santa's sleigh.

"Wow, so I am!" The tone of pride was soon forgotten as she wove this way then that way trying to lose the wolf pack below.

"Hic, hic, hic, sick, sick, sick," said a queasy Dusty.

"Uh huh, uh huh, sick, sick, sick," said Rusty, eyes rolling and tongue hanging out.

"I think you should try a little less swerving and a little more lifting before we wear husky lunch, whoot hoot."

"Oh, I'm sorry. I was getting right into this sleigh-pulling thing," she answered, slowing down. "It was fun!"

As the sled levelled out, Olive heard a groan coming from under the tarp covering the sled. "What was that?" she asked, looking over her shoulder. The canvas cover moved.

"Yup, yup, yup Akliak, Akliak, Akliak," said Dusty.

"Uh huh, uh huh, boy, boy, boy," said Rusty.

"A humankind boy?"

"Yup, yup, yup Akliak, Akliak, Akliak," said Dusty.

"Uh huh, uh huh, boy, boy, boy," repeated Rusty.

Chloe took a great hop, landed on the sled, and pulled back the canvas with her beak to reveal a young boy of about ten years old. His eyes half opened and he groaned, obviously hurt from whatever had happened out in the woods. "Why is there a humankind boy under the tarp?" Olive cried.

"Whooman, Whooman, whoot hoot!"

"He looks hurt," Olive said.

"Yup, yup, yup, wolf attack, wolf attack, wolf attack," said Dusty.

"Uh huh, uh huh, got hurt, got hurt, got hurt," said Rusty.

"So that's why you guys were out there in the forest? You were pulling...what's his name...Akliak?"

"Yup, yup, yup Akliak, Akliak, Akliak," agreed Dusty.

"Uh huh, uh huh, boy, boy, boy," yipped Rusty.

"Whoot hoot, sounds like they got into trouble with White Storm while heading back to the village. Looks like

Rusty and Dusty stayed with their master when the other dogs all ran off. Every good dog deserves a bone! Brave doggies. Whoot hoot!"

"Very brave doggies," Olive agreed. "When we find Santa, I'll be sure to let him know how brave Rusty and Dusty are. But what do we do with the boy?"

"To the village, whoot hoot."

Mrs. Claus' words of warning echoed through Olive's mind: 'Unless you are in danger, try not to fly when humans are near.' Now here she was flying with a boy riding behind her in a sleigh toward a human village. *What will Grandpapa Nick think?* At least the boy hadn't been awake until now. There was no way she was going to land unless she had to, not with White Storm and his pack of ravenous wolves waiting to tear them apart.

Up ahead between the trees, Olive could barely see roof tops with smoke puffing out of chimneys. "That must be the village. We'll be safe there," she said excitedly, hoping the wolves were even more afraid of humankind than she was. Surely they would never attack inside a village.

Suddenly, Olive slowed down and sank below the treetops like a car running out of gas. She bobbed up and down, skimming the surface of the snow and veering left and right to avoid trees once more. Her magic was running out! After exerting herself pulling the sleigh, holding up two huskies, an owl, and a human kind child, there was little left.

"This is going to get rough so hold on!" she yelled.

The wolves saw that something was wrong. It meant an opportunity to strike. With tongues hanging out, they drove harder and were close behind when the sleigh crash-landed, bouncing heavily on the trail. As soon as their paws touched the ground the dogs leapt into action, helping Olive make the mad dash to the village.

"Get them!" White Storm howled nipping at the back of the sled.

The sled and its ragtag team careened onward. Chloe hopped to the back of the sleigh and clung to the steering handle as she pecked at the head of one of White Storms minions. A couple of pecks from Chloe's razor sharp beak and the desperate wolf squealed, let go his grip, and tumbled off into a snow bank.

Another wolf snapped at Dusty who rammed the wolf off to one side using his broad shoulders.

"Pull, pull, pull, Rusty, Rusty, Rusty," shouted Dusty.

"Uh huh, uh huh, pull, pull, pull!" replied Rusty leaning into his harness and pulling with all his might.

Swerving left then right another wolf was tossed roughly, smacking into a tree after having been struck by the zigzagging sled. Both the hunters and the prey gasped for breath.

With a final effort, Olive and her companions broke away from the wolves. Then the wolves seemed to have stopped their attack all together. "Whew, good work, boys," she said feeling a surge of relief. "Wait, that's strange. Why would they give up now? They nearly had us," she said. White Storm howled the most blood-curdling howl she had ever heard. She watched as the whole wolf pack turned and skulked back into the forest.

"We made it," she said, facing the village. Then she realized why the wolves had suddenly given up. Before her stood three humans blocking their path and they had hunting rifles pointed straight at her.

Bang! Bang! Bang! The guns fired.

CHAPTER FIFTEEN
Fort Yukon

Olive ducked to dodge the bullets whizzing by her head and slammed on her brakes as hard as she could. Rusty and Dusty dug their paws into the snow to avoid skidding into the three men pointing their rifles right at them.

"Whoooooaaaaa," she yelled, swerving hard left and toppling the sled that now skidded on its side and came to an abrupt halt at the front steps of a rustic log cabin. The momentum sent Olive and the dogs sliding across the front porch and slamming them up against the front door. Dazed and confused, Olive, Rusty, Dusty, and Chloe lay piled on top of one another. A Christmas wreath had fallen from its place on the door and now circled Chloe's neck.

The three men rushed at them, rifles still pointed directly at Olive and Chloe. Olive squeezed her eyes shut, expecting the worst.

Suddenly, the front door opened and the whole pile of them fell backward into the house. Chloe shrieked and flapped up to perch on a wood beam in the rafters, the wreath still around her neck.

"There'll be no killing on my front porch!" bellowed a voice.

Olive, fighting her natural urge to flee, looked up and saw standing over them an elderly lady wearing glasses just like Grandpapa Nick. The lady had a stern face, but calm like her Grandmama Claus'. The woman had long, white hair like Grandpapa's and she wore a dress printed with tiny flowers and a leather vest made from Porcupine caribou, which was intricately decorated with coloured beads along its edges. She stepped out on the porch, putting herself between the men outside, and Olive and Chloe inside.

"But mother, we didn't know if the reindeer was taking Akliak's sled with Rusty and Dusty," one of the men answered.

Olive peered through the woman's legs. "She was coming toward you," the woman answered. "If she was taking the sled do you not think she would go the other way?"

"Yes, Mother."

"I believe this reindeer was saving Akliak from the wolves. You did see the wolves."

"Yes, Grandmother," said the lead man.

Olive felt comforted by the woman's presence but couldn't put a hoof on why. Then she realized that Christmas music was playing somewhere in the house. The tune was *Santa Claus is Coming to Town*. Somehow it calmed her and against all the warnings of Grandmama Claus and Alabaster, she didn't run.

"Mother," said one of the men respectfully, "we will not harm the reindeer." He peered at Olive. "It is not often we see a Woodland reindeer in Porcupine caribou country," he said, lowering his weapon.

"There is something special about this reindeer," the lady said looking into Olive's frightened eyes. "I sense an

133

old soul from our ancestors. I don't know why but somehow I feel connected to this animal."

"I guess she was trying to save Akliak and our missing dogs from the wolf pack we scared away," said the man.

The old woman could see the harness still around Olive's neck and with a gentle hand the lady rubbed her snout as she unfastened the harness. Olive could hear the woman's thoughts spoken directly to her. "Don't be afraid, my little one, Vadzaih. You are safe here," she said, calling Olive's name in Gwitch'in, her native tongue.

Feeling no threat from the elder, Olive immediately felt at ease and stood up, free from the dog harness. One of the hunters gaped at seeing his mother touch a deer without it sprinting away in fright. The other two men lifted the boy child out of the sled and carried him into the house under the watchful eye of Chloe, perched safely in the rafters. They laid him on the sofa and he stirred awake.

"Grandmother," he mumbled, looking up at her kindly face, "I think I was flying." He rubbed his eyes.

"He has had a blow to his head, Grandmother," said one man.

"He must still be confused," said another.

"With the wolves nipping at your heels, you were coming in really fast, Akliak. It probably seemed like you were flying. We all know that Woodland caribou cannot fly," said the third.

"We were, Grandmother, up in the air above the trees," the boy insisted putting a hand to his head where he had received a wallop while escaping the wolves.

"Now, now, I'm sure this has been very taxing day for you, Akliak," the old woman said brushing hair away from the wound. "Let me have a look at that nasty bump on your head."

The grandmother glanced at Olive. She knew the boy was telling the truth. She realised what Olive was but turned her attention back to her grandson. "Get some water and the first-aid kit," she ordered the men. "Then you boys put Rusty and Dusty back in the kennels with the other dogs and put the sleigh away. I'll see to Akliak."

"What about the reindeer and owl?" one man asked.

"Leave them; I will deal with them later. I'm sure they won't be any trouble for me," she answered.

After the men left the cabin, Chloe stepped off the rafter and flapped down to re-perched on Olive's antlers in case they might have to make a run for it. But Olive stayed right where she stood, as calm as could be.

"What happened, young man?" the old lady asked the boy.

"We were hunting when the zhoh appeared," he said, pulling himself up on the pillow. "All at once those wolves were all around us, Grandma."

"Go on."

"I guess I panicked and ran. I was so scared."

"Why did you not shoot your rifle at them?"

"Because I dropped it in the snow when made a run for it," Akliak answered.

"And the dogs?"

"They panicked too, all but Rusty and Dusty. They stayed with me and pulled the sled," he said proudly.

"The others came home hours ago, so they are safe," the grandmother told him.

"We ran and ran and would have made it but we crashed. That's the last thing I remember."

135

"Well, you are safe now so get some rest. I will make some hot soup for you and we can talk about it more in the morning."

"Thank-you, Grandma," he said, rolling over on his side. The old woman covered him with a handmade blanket and he was soon fast sleep.

"You can tell me the rest," she said turning and to a surprised Olive. "Don't pretend you cannot speak to me. I know you can. I know animals speak to each other like you do with your friend the owl. You cannot fool me."

Olive and Chloe looked at each other in disbelief. The animal world never speaks to humankind and humankind only thinks it can talk to animals but generally they get it all wrong. But they could hear this lady plainly and did not know what to do or say.

"Our people are Gwitch'in of the Athapascan nation and have lived here since Dotson'Sa, the Raven, created the world. Long ago our ancestors were able to speak to animals and animals could talk to us but over time, that ability was lost between us. I am the village shaman and elder here in Fort Yukon and have learned the old ways of our peoples so you may speak to me, Vadzaih, I will understand you."

"My grandmama said I am not supposed to speak to humankind," Olive blurted out, much to Chloe's surprise. When she realized what she had done, she tried to cover it by snorting like a wild reindeer.

"There, that wasn't so difficult was it?" the lady said. "I knew you were special from the moment I laid my eyes on you."

Olive gave up on pretending and hoped that the trust the old woman expressed was genuine. "Your knowledge of the old ways has made you wise."

"Whoot hoot, there are those whooo are wise and there are those whooo are otherwise, whoot hoot!"

"My name is Olive, and this is Chloe. May I ask what your name is, kind lady?" Olive said ignoring Chloe.

"My Gwitch'in tribal name would be too difficult to pronounce for you so you may call me Alice. Most of the village just calls me Grandmother. Now, tell me what happened out there?"

"We were soaring along heading west…" Olive began, when suddenly Chloe hopped down from her antlers and sank her talons into Olive's back. "Ow! Why did you do…um…I mean we were moving quickly, heading west to try and find Grandpapa Nick and my papa when we came upon Rusty and Dusty stuck with the sled. We stopped to try and help."

"I see…"

"Then White Storm and his Howling Dozen found us. They attacked, so I jumped into the harness and helped pull the sled out from between the rocks."

"You did a good deed for a stranger."

"Whoot hoot, you can never get dizzy from doing too many good turns!"

"I couldn't leave the two dogs. They would have been torn to pieces," Olive continued.

"How did you outrun the zhoh, White Storm?"

"Er…"

"You flew, didn't you?"

"I…"

"The only reindeer like you around these parts are Nicholas' reindeer, and I've now heard both you and Akliak say you were flying."

Feeling like a child caught in the act of mischief by her mother, Olive slumped, realizing she had been found out.

"The only way to keep a secret is not to tell it, whoot hoot!"

"I know, but she…"

"There is a reason I am the village shaman here in Fort Yukon," Alice said.

"We are in Fort Yukon? Is this Alaska?"

"Yes, this is Alaska the land of the Athapaskan nation."

"Yahoo! We finally made it!"

"I also know things happen for a reason. Reindeer do not just show up out of nowhere. So tell me why you are here, little one?"

"I'm on a mission to find Santa. He has not returned from his Christmas Eve journey. Grandmama Claus sent me to find him and the rest of the reindeer, including my papa."

"Ah, I see. So Santa Claus is missing."

"Grandmama and Alabaster think Santa returns to the North Pole through Alaska. We did not see him in the arctic so we figured he's somewhere in Alaska."

"Well, for you helping my grandson and the dogs, you deserve a reward. Now tell me what can I do for you?"

"We have heard not one word that he crash landed so we think something awful has happened to him. I keep hearing of a bad person called the Blizzard Wizard and I am wondering if he had anything to do with Santa's disappearance?"

"Yes, we know of this wretched soul and he could very well be mixed up in all of this. Evil deeds like a fire can be hidden for a short time, but smoke cannot. He roams these lands like a tortured character creating all kinds of mayhem."

"Why would he do such things?"

"We of the Gwitch'in people believe that one cannot be admitted to enter into the afterlife unless your heart and mind are completely empty. Your soul will be forever stuck on earth to roam as a spirit.

"How does he do that?"

"One must leave all possessions behind to pass the test to enter. Not just the physical ones but spiritual and emotional ones as well. Especially hateful ones. I believe this Blizzard Wizard still walks this earth and cannot move on until he rids himself of his heavy heart or the spirit that has possessed him."

"Wow, that's heavy! Whoot hoot!"

"When we die we leave behind all that we have and take with us all that we are, whoot hoot."

"Very true, wise owl," the grandmother said.

"How do we find this wizard?" Olive asked the old woman.

"He is rumoured to live in a cave high in the glacier of the great mountain known as Denali."

"How do we get there?"

"It will do you no good. His evil has grown too strong and is too powerful for a little reindeer like you."

"But I must find Grandpapa Nicholas and my papa, Prancer!"

"If you must then you must. I don't recommend you try but I will tell you how. You must travel over the White Mountains into the Tanana peoples' land and onward to the next mountain range. Look for the tallest mountain.

That would be Denali. However, I fear for you if you take this path before you are ready."

"What should I do?"

"For now you must rest while I put some healing ointment on the owl's injured wing. While you sleep I will talk to our ancestors and elders of the village to see if there is anything we can do."

Dark shadows filtered through the ice and Saint Nicholas could see movement of someone or something pacing madly back and forth. "Who is that?" his brain screamed, "and what does he want with me?"

"I have you, Santa Claus!" he heard the muffled voice say, through the ice. "After all these years, I finally have you!" the wicked voice crowed in a raspy gasp of victory. "You will be my prisoner forever! Hee, hee, hee!"

"But why?" Santa pleaded in the best mumble he could utter.

"Because I hate Christmas!" was the snapping reply.

"Oh dear, that is sad," Santa responded.

"Sad! This isn't sad. It's the happiest day of my life!" And again the evil spectre laughed in the most hideous way.

"But why?"

"Now, there will never be another Christmas! Never!"

"You obviously know me but I didn't have the pleasure of getting your name," Santa said as politely as he could.

"I am the Blizzard Wizard! Ruler of Storms," the menace bellowed, his voice echoing through the cavern.

"What do you plan to do with us?" Santa inquired.

"You will be a frozen mural in my wall! My trophy! My greatest triumph displayed in ice for all to see!" the voice howled in glee. "Well, perhaps not for all to see. In fact, I think I prefer just me!"

"Surely you don't mean that," Santa said.

"Santa Claus will never ride his sleigh again, will never deliver toys to those, those ungrateful children, and never bring happiness or hope to anyone ever again!"

This is not good at all, Santa thought as a single tear slowly trickled from the corner of his eye and froze on his cheek. "Surely you don't mean that?"

"But I do, I do!"

"How could anyone not want Santa to visit all the children? Some children would never get a toy at all if it wasn't for Santa's visit."

"Isn't that too bad!" the being sneered. "And do you know what's best of all?"

"I can't imagine anything worse."

"No one will ever again sing those silly songs about you or your reindeer, ever!" His voice had reached a fevered pitch then with a flicker, the light disappeared and Santa was left in complete darkness. *My, how sad. I think he really believes those hateful words,* he thought, *I can't imagine anyone feeling this much pain.*

Unable to do anything about his dire situations, his thoughts turned to his loved ones at home. *I hope Carol and the elves are okay,* he thought. *I am sure they must be very worried by now.*

Rudolf and the other reindeer had heard the wickedness in their captor's voice and it filled them with fear. They knew they were completely helpless. Their natural senses told them to flee but they remained stuck, as though in concrete, and couldn't so much as twitch a muscle. Not one of them could believe it was true.

In all the centuries they had pulled Santa's sleigh they had never been in such a tight spot. Their only comfort was in knowing that at least Santa was there with them. He had always led them out of trouble in the past but this was different than anything they had experienced before.

CHAPTER SIXTEEN
Change of Direction

Olive woke the following morning on a bed of straw someone had made for her on the front porch of Alice's house. She sensed a presence close by and opened one eye. Startled, she saw ten-year-old Akliak with his face no more than a breath away from hers.

"I dreamt that I was flying yesterday," he declared staring into her eyes. "And you were pulling the sleigh like Santa's reindeer."

Olive stood up, said nothing, and started to eat the feed that had been thoughtfully laid out for her by the old lady.

"I could swear I was flying. Can you fly?"

Olive continued to pretend she did not understand the boy and to act like any other reindeer.

"Only Santa's reindeer know how to fly. Are you one of them?" he peppered. "Really, are you one? Are you Dasher…" He stared at Olive intently for any sign, "or Dancer? Prancer?" Olive's ears flicked up but she didn't stop eating. "Vixen? Donner…"

"Stop bothering the reindeer," Alice interrupted, stepping out the front door. "Just be thankful she saved you from the wolves." Strains of the song, *Rudolf the Red Nosed Reindeer,* wafted out from behind her.

"Yes, Grandmother, but I really thought I was flying."

"You were confused after the thump on your head."

"But…"

"And it must have seemed like you were flying because you all came in so fast into the village with the wolves chasing close behind." She knew Olive had a very important mission to carry out and if she told her grandson the truth about the reindeer, he would want to keep her as a pet. Before long the rest of the villagers would know who she really was, and then who knew what they would want to do with her?

"Maybe you're right, Grandmother, but I was so sure." His shoulders slumped. His dreams overnight had convinced him he had been riding in a sleigh with one of Santa's reindeer in the lead and Rusty and Dusty following. It was a dream any child in the world would love to be true.

"If you are feeling better, there's a rifle you left behind somewhere out there," Alice said tossing her head toward the backwoods. "You'd better take the dogs and find it before somebody else does."

"Yes, Grandmother. I'll hook up the team and head out. I have a good idea where it will be." Akliak, got up, scratched Olive behind her ear and whispered, "Thank-you, reindeer, for saving me." He paused then added, "And I know you can fly." Then he headed toward the dog kennels.

"Be a lot more careful this time," Alice called after him.

"I will, Grandmother."

"And watch out for those wolves!" she shouted.

"Yes, Grandmother," was the distant reply as he disappeared around the corner of the house.

Once the boy was out of sight, Alice faced Olive and her companion, Chloe, who was back on her familiar perch on Olive's antlers "Now, let's talk about your situation, my reindeer friend."

The old woman sat down on the porch chair and motioned Olive to come close. Holding Olive's lightly by the chin, she whispered so that only she could hear, "I talked to the other elders last night and they have heard stories that on Christmas morning before dawn, there was a raging storm in the south."

"Yes, Grandmother," Olive said. It felt more fitting to call her that than shaman or Alice.

"And that a mysterious blue light bolted up from the great Denali mountain high into the sky."

"What do you think the blue light was for?"

"That is the same question I had, so I spent the night in prayer and talking with our ancestors. I'm afraid your worst fears are correct."

"What do you mean, Grandmother?"

"The ancestors believe it was a black magic spell. Evil cast by a spirit that has not passed into the afterlife. They think it was directed toward your Grandpapa Nicholas and now holds him."

"Holds him?"

"Imprisoned. A spell so strong that even the wondrous Santa Claus with all his magic cannot break it."

Tears stung Olive's eyes. "Now what do I do? Even if I find him at the large mountain, how will I set him free?" she whispered sadly.

"You must break the spell and to do that you need to free the heart of this…what did you call him? The Blizzard Wizard?"

"Yes, the Blizzard Wizard."

"This wizard has to see his path to the afterlife before he can let go of all his anger and pain."

"A grouch never does what he's told until he dies, whoot hoot!" Chloe chortled.

"How do I do that?" Olive asked, ignoring Chloe. She was unconvinced that she had any power to make this happen.

"You must find something or someone from his past that will pull him out of his rage. Do you know how he became a wandering spirit?"

Olive recalled the story Sly the fox had told her about the wizard. "We met an Arctic fox on Banks Island."

"Whoot hoot, in the ocean off Banks Island," Chloe corrected.

"Yes, yes, we saved him from some orcas, but that's another story. Anyway his name is Sly and he said that the Blizard Wizzard was a sea captain who froze to death on Christmas day."

"Ah, sounds like one of the ships that were trying to discover the Northwest Passage. Many of those ships froze up there as they tried to find their way through the numerous islands. They tried to sail from the big sea they call the Atlantic to western big sea they call Pacific."

"That's what Bruce the Christmoose said!" Olive cried.

"Bruce who?"

"Bruce the Christmoose. He's a moose in training to be a Santa's Helper and wears Christmas decorations on his antlers."

"He is, I mean, he does?"

"Yes. I know it sounds funny but the Christmas spirit does strange things to people, and animals!"

"That is so true. Fort Yukon loves Christmas and Santa's visits every year. Does Bruce the Christmoose know where to find this frozen ship?"

"I don't know but he knew of the legend."

"Do you know where to find him to ask?"

"That's a problem. We didn't find him; he found us out there somewhere in the woods. I'm afraid I'd get lost looking for him if I went back out there."

"Whoot hoot, something lost is always found in the last place you look."

"But I have no idea how to get back to Mizz's cave after being chased by White Storm and his Howling Dozen again."

"Mizz?" the old woman asked.

"Mizz the Grizz. She's a grizzly bear who was hibernating for the winter in her den."

"You hid in a grizzly bear's den while she was in it!?" Alice said, astonished. "That was a brave thing to do."

"Whoot hoot, there's a fine line between bravery and foolishness," Chloe chirped, while Alice nodded in agreement.

"It was Bruce's idea and it seemed like a good one until the wolves found us and decided to take on a full grown moose. That's when the entire ruckus really got started. Unfortunately, Mizz woke up in a bad mood so Bruce, the wolves, Chloe, and I all took off as fast as rockets. That's the last place we saw Bruce the Christmoose."

"A grizzly bear's den," Alice said, shaking her head. "That is amazing."

"It was either that or be eaten by the wolves."

"Well, finding Bruce seems out of the question," she murmured, thinking out loud. "I wonder if this Sly friend of yours knows where the ship is?"

"Perhaps. He didn't tell us that, but he knew that Blizzard Wizard was once a sea captain."

"Maybe if you can find the ship, you might find something on it that will help the Blizzard Wizard get free of his evil spell and pass on to the afterlife."

"Do you think so?"

"It's all we've got. As brave as you are, I don't think you will be able free your grandpapa on your own. You need something to help you."

"Like what?"

"You'll know it when you see it."

Olive swung her head from side to side. "I just don't know what to do," she wailed. "What if I can't find the ship or find anything on it that might help?"

"Whoot hoot, always take plenty of time to make a snap decision," Chloe chimed in, trying to help.

"Chloe, I don't want to make a stupid mistake. Either we carry on or go back north. I wish I could talk to my papa. He'd know what to do."

"Whoot hoot, a reindeer that never makes a mistake gets awfully tired of doing nothing!"

"Then it's better to do something than nothing at all." Olive stood up straight. "Let's go find this ship." Then she thought for a moment. "Which way out of here is north?"

The old lady pointed and said, "That-a-way."

Olive was about to lift off when the old woman stopped her.

"You can't take off from here. The whole village will see you and especially Akliak who will make a big fuss if anyone sees you fly."

"Good point. We wouldn't want to create a fuss, would we, Chloe?"

"Whoot hoot, if you prove that reindeer can fly you spoil a good rumour," Chloe chortled.

"I suggest you wait and rest a little while longer so Akliak will be well on his way and the rest of the men have gone hunting on their snowmobiles. Then you can head into the woods and take off from there."

While Olive rested on the front porch she endured the many stares from villagers who could not believe their eyes. Rumours had rippled through the village since the previous night. No one could remember the last time a Woodland caribou had visited the village and hung about. Grandmother's status of a shaman was re-confirmed. After all, who else could have enough power to entice a reindeer and an owl to stay so long?

Once the street was quiet and the people had gone indoors, Alice stepped out of her house. In her hand she held a leather pouch. "I have something for your journeys."

"A gift for me?" Olive asked excitedly.

"Whoot hoot, friendship is the best gift," Chloe hooted.

"That is true, you old wise owl, but I think this may help you both."

"Watch who you call old, whoot hoot." Chloe ruffled her feathers but had a twinkle in her eye.

Alice opened the pouch to reveal a compass on a long leather tether. Olive had never seen anything like it before, nor had Chloe. "Oh, thank-you, Grandmother. Er…what is it?"

"It is called a compass."

"What does it do?" Olive peered at the face of the apparatus.

"It helps you find your way. I sense you get lost easily."

"You can say that again! Whoot hoot."

Olive overlooked Chloe's comment.

"How does this thing work, Grandmother?" asked Olive.

"See the dial that has an N, E, S, and E? That means, north, east, south, and west."

"I see," she answered, examining the dial.

"Now see the red arrow? It always points north so you turn the dial so the red arrow points to the N. That way you know which way north, south, east, and west is."

"Awesome!"

"Whoot hoot, whoot hoot," Chloe twittered, flapping her wings.

Alice hung the compass around Olive's neck, struggling to get the lace over her antlers. "Now you won't be able to lose that so easily."

"Thank-you, Grandmother! What a wonderful gift!"

Alice smiled at Olive and Chloe. "I think it's that time," she said, stroking Olive's soft ear until it tickled the reindeer. "Travel north until you reach the Arctic Ocean, turn east until you find Banks Island. Your friend Sly should be easy to find."

"Thank-you, Grandmother."

"Now off you go." She wiped a tear from her eye. "Head into the woods, and have a safe journey."

CHAPTER SEVENTEEN
Old Friend Sly

Mrs. Claus and Alabaster had received the good news that Olive was still searching and that Bruce the Christmoose had saved her from the wolves but they were desperate to hear any news of Nicholas and the reindeer team.

"I hope they are safe, wherever they are," Mrs. Claus fretted. "I can't imagine not having my Nicholas around." She had worn a patch in carpet by the window from pacing back and forth.

"As each day passes I become more worried than the day before," Alabaster said, frowning. He was having a tough time reading the many letters still coming in for next year. "There haven't been any reports of the reindeer roaming or Santa's sleigh being seen."

"I know Olive is doing her best but we can't just sit here," Mrs. Claus fussed, sitting down to sip her cold tea.

"There must be something we can do?" Alabaster claimed, giving up on the letters.

"As much as I don't like to leave the North Pole, we may have no choice." She was finally prepared to accept the unthinkable.

"That will put us at risk of being discovered," Alabaster reminded her.

"I think we have to take the risk to help Olive," she replied, wringing her hands. "Someone has to go to the cities."

"I'll have the spare sleigh ready to go and hook up Rollo and Bingo." Alabaster got up from his desk but Mrs. Claus stopped him.

"Do you think they are ready?"

"I know they are young—especially Bingo—but they are all we have. We will be with them so we can keep an eye on them."

Mrs. Claus nodded. "That's true. Who will we leave in charge here?"

"I think Noel can handle things while we're gone."

With Olive looking in the wilderness and avoiding humankind, they decided to don disguises and visit the towns and cities in Alaska that would be on the route Santa would have travelled. To hide Alabaster's small, elf size, they decided he would pose as Carol's grandson and would wear a green, knitted toque to cover his pointed ears and a blue winter coat like Alaskan children wear. Mrs. Claus dressed in a red winter parka with a white faux fur collar, and pulled on her snow boots.

Looking at each other standing in front of the full-length mirror, they surveyed the strange looking clothes. "Do you think we'll pass inspection?" Alabaster said turning first one way then the other.

"It will have to do," she replied. "Now let's be off."

Using the last of the magic dust to propel them they rode in the back-up sleigh, now painted black and with all bells removed to avoid recognition. With Rollo and Bingo in the front wearing plain harnesses, the new team zoomed across the Arctic with the wind at their backs. They stayed low to reduce the risk of being discovered by watchful eyes both above and below.

They would have never have attempted such a journey if the situation hadn't become desperate. They both knew Nicholas would have never approved, even if it were to save him. He had carefully protected his secret for nearly two thousand years and would never have wanted it revealed.

To save time, the sleigh did not take the course Santa would have taken; they preferred instead to take a direct route. Their first stop was the hospital at Bethel to ask around for any reports of a sleigh crash, reindeer injuries, or a hospitalised jolly old man in a coma.

"I'm sorry Mrs. Claus, there are no reports of a Nicholas Claus being admitted into this hospital," said the admission clerk to the disappointed but strange-looking strangers.

"Are you sure?" she pleaded, "and please call me Carol."

"Yes, ma'am, I mean, Carol. I have checked the Admissions List twice. I see no Nick or Nicholas, no Claus or Saints," he replied.

"What about a John Doe? Or just someone admitted wearing a Santa suit?" Alabaster asked in his best child's voice.

"No one of that name, or unknown name, or wearing a red suit." The clerk looked quizzically at Alabaster upon hearing the funny high-pitched voice. This kid looked different than the regular kids in Bethel. "In fact, we have never admitted anyone close to that description." After seeing the disappointment in their faces he suggested, "Have you checked with the police?"

"Yes, that was the first place we checked and they suggested coming here," Carol replied. "Well, thank you for your time."

The same message was repeated at institutions in Nome, Anchorage, Fairbanks, and finally at the last stop on their way home, Prudhoe Bay.

"Well, that's that," Alabaster said resigning himself to the bad news.

Disappointed and running low on magic dust they decided to head back and once again place their fading hopes in Olive coming through.

"It was a good idea, Alabaster, so don't get down on yourself," Mrs. Claus said as the sleigh lifted into the night sky. "We still have Olive…I hope."

"At least we tried," Alabaster said sadly.

Carol and Alabaster zoomed back to the North Pole in a blur as the magic dust steadily drained from the hourglass with each mile they travelled. Rollo and Bingo had never travelled such distances and were starting to labour.

"I know you're tired, little ones, but we have to keep moving." Carol called out to them.

"No worries, Grandmama. We'd do anything to help Grandpapa Nick," Rollo panted, his coat now glistening in sweat.

They crossed over the Beaufort Sea and onto the Arctic Ocean without detection by any human and were relieved when they saw the enchanted dome up ahead.

Once through the enchanted curtain they could see the lights of home ahead as the last few grains of magic dust drained from the hourglass. Their momentum barely kept them aloft as Rollo and Bingo pulled harder and harder.

"I don't think we're going to make it," Alabaster shouted.

"Mush, Rollo, mush Bingo," Mrs. Claus urged the young reindeer.

Fearing the worst, Alabaster covered his eyes as they approached the sleigh entrance but Rollo and Bingo somehow found a burst of energy and made a final terrific leap. "Hold on!" Carol hollered as they skidded into the launch bay. She and Alabaster heaved back as hard as they could on the reins as Rollo and Bingo dug in their hooves. With it swerving wildly, Rollo and Bingo managed to get the sleigh turned just in time. The sleigh came to a halt just before smacking into the double doors leading into the packing room.

"That was close!" Alabaster gasped, wiping his brow.

"Thanks to Rollo and Bingo. We couldn't have done it without them."

"I will make sure they get an extra treat tonight."

"Make it two," Mrs. Claus added.

High in the glacier of Mount Denali, the shadowy grey spectre darkened the mouth of the ice cave once more. He admired his long-awaited, prized trophy still frozen in ice like a mural painting one goes to admire at the Louvre in Paris. His imprisoned masterpiece had taken years to carefully prepare for, to calculate and plan the precise spot to be at the exact time for him to capture the symbol of all his hatred: jolly old Saint Nicholas!

Under the soft glow of a lantern, Santa saw the vague shadow through the ice surrounding him. The figure appeared to be gloating over his treasure. Unable to move and unable to speak clearly, Nicholas groaned in protest and managed to ask the phantom one simple question: "Why?"

The apparition whispered his response in deep, raspy speech. "I see your face, Nicholas. I see what you are asking so I will enlighten you. You are my prize because you represent all that is good in this cruel world, all that is nice, sweet, and all giving, forever sprinkled with hope and charity. Father Christmas! Bah! What a line of poppycock." Santa sensed the deep pain in his voice as the spectre continued. "But I was deceived by this humanity. There is no such thing as humanity."

Santa managed to mumble, "But there is good in the world."

"Humans are critical, cynical, cruel, and full of hatred and lies," he hissed. "They do not love anybody but themselves and their own self-interests. They care not for mankind, charity, or peace. Only money gives them a temporary thrill. God must be so disappointed in his greatest achievement: mankind.

Through the ice, Nicholas saw the grimace on the hooded spirit. He tried to show sympathy with just a look and would have comforted the spirit if he were free. Tears always turn to smiles when children of all ages can feel love when they're held in the arms of someone honestly expressing it.

"Oh yes, once, I too shared your sense of adventure and love of life, Nicholas. The fairy tale that all would turn out how it should, that people would always do the right thing, and the world would be a wonderful place to exist. But alas, I know this is all a lie," the specter murmured.

Santa gazed at him in disbelief.

"Don't look at me with that face because I know it is true! All I found was misery; that nothing is ever fair; promises are broken and wasted on deceit. No one cares and they take great pleasure in laughing at my folly. I have vowed to make everyone forever feel only pain, just as I do, to haunt this cruel world where I was cheated, a world where I find no peace and will give none."

Nicholas was appalled at how one could think and feel the way this spirit did. He had never known such scorn in his heart and had always shown in everything he did that the world is so much better place with love and care for one another, just as God's Son had asked us to do two thousand years ago. Happiness for Nicholas had always been a cure for emptiness and the joy of giving had always been a better reward than the receiving of gifts. The spectre's belief was such a strange concept to Santa Claus and that his only thought was, *how can I help relieve this poor soul's pain?*

The daring voyagers sneaked out of Fort Yukon when the coast appeared clear and hurried into the shadows of the woods. It seemed weird and wonderful to Olive to be amongst humankind. It was something she had never experienced before. She had never met an actual person other than Grandpapa Nicholas and Grandmama Carol. While had been exciting for her, she definitely sensed the danger that Mrs. Claus had warned her about, but she also felt the goodness and warmth from the old woman. *Humans are so complicated*, she thought.

Olive made her way down a trail, off the beaten track, and found a small clearing in the woods outside of Fort Yukon. All the while she kept a watchful eye out for

White Storm and his menacing pack, and also the prying eyes of one special child who didn't need any more proof that Olive was one of Santa's reindeer.

"Ready Chloe?"

"Hope for the best and be ready for the worst, whoot hoot!" the owl replied.

Using her new gift from the shaman to guide her and with Chloe once again perched in her familiar place atop her antlers, Olive lifted off and headed north, thankful she was clear of Fort Yukon and all its scuttlebutt about a strange visitor protected by the shaman. She had been nervous in a town of humankind hunters carrying the scent of death and wearing the skins of her cousins. *How can anyone wear the hide of another animal*, she wondered with a shudder. As far as she knew, only humankind did such strange things.

She would miss the warm kindness of the old woman called Alice, the Gwitch'in elder, and Akliak, the boy she saved and who knew who she really was. Rusty and Dusty, the huskies, had gentle hearts and would have given their lives to protect the boy. That impressed Olive very much. But she would absolutely not miss the vicious and relentless White Storm and his Howling Dozen.

For Olive, it was comforting to once again cross the tree line into the familiar barren snow of the arctic. Having lived at the North Pole all her life this was the only scenery she had ever known. The temperature had now dipped at least twenty degrees once more, to the torment of Chloe. She had become used to the slightly warmer temperatures of Fort Yukon.

Once again, the cruel cold wind flared up and it bit fiercely on their ears and stung their eyes as they flew northward. Below, Olive watched caribou running, arctic rabbits scurrying away, and muskoxen snorting as the determined duo approached overhead. Staying low but with speed, they covered the tundra landscape swiftly. There was no time to waste if they were to get to Banks Island before morning. Evening turned into darkness, sunlight turned into moonlight, and stars glittered before Olive saw a set of lights in the distance. She knew these lights indicated where humankind gathered to make their nests.

"Whoot, hoot, Inuvik, Inuvik," Chloe hooted.

"I beg your pardon?"

"Inuvik town where hunters live, whoot hoot," she squawked.

Not wanting to risk another encounter with hunters and to stay out of sight, Olive veered widely around the town's glow and kept safely in the shadows of night. The last thing she needed was to be shot at again or captured.

"I hope this will be worth coming back all this way," Olive lamented.

"Every road to success has a couple of flats along the way, whoot hoot."

Once past Inuvik the land below her disappeared and she now flew over the coast of the Beaufort Sea. Floating icebergs dotted the sea but thankfully, there were no signs of that pod of orcas. Remembering her journey south, Olive knew it wouldn't be long before they reached their destination and she hoped that Sly would still be there.

As they forged ahead, Olive's movements started to labour. She had never flown such long distances before in one jaunt. Using her compass, she adjusted her course every so often and before she knew it, she saw craggy shores of Banks Island ahead.

"There it is!" she cried, seeing the rocky terrain. *This compass thing actually worked*, she thought.

By the time she reached the island and landed, Olive felt completely exhausted and out of breath. They were at the exact spot she had been when they had saved Sly from the orcas. She hoped that Sly might still be there, or at least close by. But her hopes were dashed when all she saw was the barren snow covered land smudged with outcrops of gravel and rocks for as far as the eye could see. There was no sign of Sly.

"We will have to look for him in the morning," she wheezed. "I'm so tired. I really don't know how Papa and my uncles can do this every year, and they go all around the whole world in one night!"

"Practice makes perfect…with a little magic dust, whoot hoot!"

"I guess so."

"If anyone could do it, everyone would be doing it. Whoot hoot."

"I feel I have run a double marathon race for the first time! I can't breathe, my legs are all wobbly, and every muscle feels like it's on fire."

"That's why everybody doesn't do it, whoot hoot."

"I guess you're right," she said, finding a place to rest behind a sizable rock, sheltered from the wind.

"There's a fine line between bravery and insanity, whoot hoot!"

"Oh hush, Chloe. That's enough."

"Only trying to help, whoot hoot!"

"There's a fine line between help and hindrance," Olive retorted.

"Oh touché, wise one."

Olive nestled her body against a curve in the rock, curled up around Chloe, and sharing each other's warmth, they were soon fast asleep.

In the fog of sleep, Olive thought she felt something small hit her head. Thinking it was something blown by the wind, she didn't open her eyes and drifted back into slumber. But when the second object hit her on the nose, she opened her eyes with a start, looking around to see what was disturbing her wondrous sleep.

"Finally," said a voice behind her.

"What?" she said, startled.

"I thought you'd never wake up." Sly sat on top of the rock behind her with a pile of small stones beside him.

"Oh, hello, Sly. It's great to see you. We had such a long journey to get here yesterday, I guess I was too tired to hear you."

"It's a good job it was me and not the wolves or a bear. They would have torn you to pieces by now."

"You're probably right. I'll try to keep an eye out. We have had our close calls with White Storm and his Howling Dozen down at the tree line."

"Whoot hoot, close call! Any closer and we'd be down his throat!"

"That bad, eh? Well, it looks like you made it through, all in one piece. You're lucky; many others haven't."

"I wouldn't want to try our luck again," Olive told him.

"The only sure thing about luck is that it will always change, whoot hoot."

"Always keep your wits about you, that's what I always say," Sly advised. "Slip in, slip out, before anyone sees you."

"Hmm…and you wonder why foxes get a bad reputation," Chloe said, raising a feathered eyebrow.

"Look at me, I'm as white as the driven snow," Sly said, innocently fluffing up his thick fur coat to hide his guilty grin.

"Whoot hoot, a reputation always looks worse when you try to decorate it and make it look good!"

Sly changed the subject. "Anyway, what brings you back here? Are you on your way home? Did you find Santa?"

"No, we did not find Santa or my papa. We came back to find you."

"Me? Why would you want to come back all this way to see me?"

"We believe the Blizzard Wizard is involved."

"The Blizzard Wizard! I hope he has nothing to do with it. You're really in trouble if that is true."

"We met an old woman in Fort Yukon who is a shaman with the Gwitch'in people and she thinks the Blizzard Wizard is a trapped soul who cannot pass on to the afterlife."

"Shaman?"

"Something like a spiritual leader, I think."

"There's more to life than just life! Whoot hoot."

"She thinks the Blizzard Wizard has done something to Santa and the reindeer."

"Humankind is so complicated," Sly said, shaking his head.

"About the time when Santa would have been returning they saw a mysterious blue light flash up in the sky and that could only come from the Blizzard Wizard."

"Wow, that's crazy! How do you think you can free Santa and your papa if he has that kind of power?"

"That's what she said. She says we need help."

"What kind of help do you think I can give, Olive? I have trouble finding lunch let alone having special powers to stop a wizard."

"She says if we can find something that will ease his hatred and the pain he carries deep in his heart, his soul can be released into the afterlife."

"Okay…that sounds pretty heavy." Sly paused then asked, "How can little ol' me help find whatever it is?"

"It was something you said when we last saw you. You said his ship was frozen in the ice near here. We need to find that ship."

"You'll mean the old wooden ship called the Red Eyed Raven."

"Whatever ship this Blizzard Wizard came from. I think you said it was near here frozen in the ice."

"Well, it kinda is." Sly shrugged his skinny shoulders.

"What do you mean 'kinda'?"

"It's northeast of here, past the frozen strait."

"That can't be too hard to find, could it?" Olive said readying for take-off. "Let's go!"

"And hidden in a small inlet on the north side of Melville Island," he said then added sheepishly, "or so they tell me."

Olive stopped in her tracks. "Or so they tell you? Does that mean you've never been there before?"

"Why would I ever want to go find a ship full of ghosts?"

"Hmmm," Olive supposed. "I wouldn't either."

"Another flat in our road to success, whoot hoot," Chloe quipped.

"I didn't come all this way to give up, Chloe, so we have to repair the flat," Olive answered. Sly gave her a funny look.

"My cousins calls the inlet Hell's Finger because of all the moaning and groaning they hear coming from there," Sly offered, hoping it would help.

"Whoot hoot, hell is heaven's junkyard," Chloe chirped.

"Sly, do you think you can show us the way?" Olive asked.

"It will take forever with me leading the way on the ice," Sly protested.

"But you're our last hope to save Santa," Olive begged, batting her eyelashes and gazing at him with her big, brown eyes.

"Okay, okay. Stop it with those eyes. But it's gonna take a while on foot. I'm just little, you know."

"I thought you could ride on my back like Chloe."

"Whoot hoot," Chloe protested, "I know I'm supposed to keep my friends close and my enemies even closer but this is ridiculous." She jumped up to the highest antler. She knew what Olive was going to say.

"Oh, Chloe, Sly is our friend and we really need his help. Right Sly? Chloe has nothing to worry about."

"Nothing to worry about at all," he said, giving Chloe an evil grin and waggling his eyebrows. This made her even more nervous.

"Whoot hoot, whoot hoot!" Chloe squawked.

"All aboard." Olive had always wanted to say that.

"Don't worry, Chloe. I'll be good," Sly said as innocently as he could muster then jumped off the rock onto Olive's back.

"Whoot hoot, I've heard there is some good in everybody, but in your case it is a little harder to find."

"Whoah," Sly cried trying to get his footing on the reindeer's frosty hair. With his paws slipping each time he tried to stand he decided to sit. "As I said before, Chloe, not all foxes are bad. Some just have a bad reputation."

Olive hovered above the ground. "So, Sly, which way do we go?"

"That-a-way," Sly said raising his paw and pointing northeast.

CHAPTER EIGHTEEN
Yo Ho Ho

Re-energized after her good night's sleep, Olive was able to make good time crossing over barren Banks Island. By flying low, Sly was able to recognize the way, keeping them on track as they entered the icy strait. Sly continued to feel unsteady riding on Olive's back but once he got used to the height off the ground he thought it was actually pretty cool to be flying. He couldn't wait to tell his family when he got home that he actually flew on a reindeer. And not just any reindeer, but one of Santa's reindeer!

The farther north they went and the closer they got to the Arctic Circle, the snow grew ever deeper, making it harder for Sly to keep them on track. With Olive stopping to use her compass and Sly hopping off every now and then to survey the ground, they managed find the trail and get back on their way.

The up-heaved ice below looked like a landslide; all scrunched up and blocking the passage Olive knew to be the McClure Strait. Loud cracking sounds echoed from the ice as it shuddered and groaned. Olive could see how old wooden ships could have been crushed in such conditions.

When they reached the shores of Melville Island, the first thing Olive noticed was a herd of Peary caribou and two muskoxen scrounging for what little lichen and moss they could dig from under the deep snow. She wondered how these animals survived all this time in such barren and hostile surroundings. Somehow they managed to get enough to eat and raise their families. She thought of the North Pole with all its comforts and felt so thankful. She promised herself never again to complain when receiving the same old suppers and, especially to cherish the treats Santa sneaked in when he thought Grandmama Claus wasn't looking.

"I see you're lost in thought, whoot hoot. Are you in unfamiliar territory?"

"Ha ha, very funny Chloe. I was just thinking how lucky I am when I see how my cousins have to survive in the wilderness."

"You don't know the half of it," exclaimed Sly. "Try raising a family and see how tough it is, especially one as large as mine!"

Next she saw the wreckage of a large aeroplane half buried in the ice that the fierce winds had exposed and would cover again with snow when they returned. The mangled pieces of metal strewn all over looked as though the plane had crashed many years before.

"I really hope whoever went down in that plane survived and was rescued," Olive said though she didn't feel very positive about it.

"Whoot hoot, I hope they didn't just rely on hope."

"I wonder if they were heading to where I found you, Chloe?"

"Humankind, were never made to fly, whoot hoot."

"Nor foxes," said Sly, still feeling uncomfortable not having his feet on the ground.

"You'd thought someone would have picked up the trash up by now."

"Humankind leaves trash all over the place," Sly said scornfully. "I can't tell you how many times my cousins have caught their legs in metal contraptions humans have left behind."

"That is not trash. Those are called traps, Sly, made to catch animals like you, whoot hoot!"

"You mean they leave them there on purpose? Ooooh, those scoundrels!" Sly said angrily. "No wonder animals don't trust them!"

"Nor you, whoot hoot," Chloe chirped with a grin.

Onward they went, using the moon and the reflection off the snow to see where they were headed. The landscape all looked the same until they reached the other side of the island. There they saw a hidden cove covered with ice.

"This is it!" cried Sly. "I'm sure this is it."

"At last. Now let's find that ship," Olive announced. Suddenly there was a loud cracking noise coming from the ice.

"Do you hear that?" asked Sly, using his sharp hearing. "It sounds like singing."

Olive made her way toward the sound. The closer they got, the clearer they could hear the voices heartily singing.

Captain Blizzard became a wizard
Stabbed the first mate in the gizzard, sang a raspy solo voice, answered stridently by the rowdy crew.

Yo-ho-ho, and a bottle of rum! the solo voice continued.
Ran away like a green-eyed lizard
Off the yardarm in a blizzard.

The voices of the others rang out:
 Yo-ho-ho, and a bottle of rum!
Thirteen souls left to survive
What put to sea with seventy-five.
Yo-ho-ho, and a bottle of rum!
Now we wait for our souls to save
So we can return to our frozen graves
Yo-ho-ho, and a bottle of rum!'
The crew followed with a rousing round of laughter.

Olive landed on the crest of the hill above it and looked in wondrous awe down at the old wooden ship under the glow of the moonlight. They stared, not quite sure they believed what their eyes were telling them. There below, highlighted by the rays of the moon, entangled in the unrelenting grip of ice, lay the wooden ship, half on its side with its red keel glowing. Its ragged rope rigging hung draped in ice and its three masts were still intact, all except the tip of the main.

Olive could see ghostly figures stumbling aimlessly around on the deck as though in a trance. "This looks scary," she whispered.

"Whoot hoot, bravery is somewhere between the heart and mind."

"You have that right, Chloe. My head says run but my heart wants to save Grandpapa and my papa."

"The bigger the head the smaller the heart and you certainly don't have a big head, whoot hoot."

"Thank you, Chloe, I guess that makes the choice for me. You guys stay here and I'll go in alone."

"Whoot hoot, I haven't come this far to be left out. I'd sooner my chances with ghosts than..."

"I get it. I always get it," said Sly. "Can't trust the sly old fox, right? Same old story, same old, same old." His slumping shoulders told Chloe how much he thought she could trust him.

"Whoot hoot, no, no, my dear friend. I meant I'd sooner my chances with ghosts than let Olive go in alone."

Sly sat up straighter. "Oh, that's nice," was all he managed to blurt out.

"Sly, you stay here and keep an eye on things, just in case," ordered Olive. "I don't know what to expect, and if anything goes wrong I'll need somebody to get help."

Sly looked around at the lonely and desolate surroundings. There was nothing to his left or right, or behind, and in front, only a ship that had been lost for over two hundred years and filled only with ghosts. "Get help? Where would I get help?"

Seeing the bewildered look on Sly's face, Olive said, "Go to the North Pole, of course. Grandmama Claus will know what to do."

"Oh, okay. Got it," he said, as he watched Olive float down toward the ship and out of earshot. His smile disappeared. "The North Pole? You've got to be kidding! I'm just a little fox, I have a family, I, I…" Then he gave up the protest. No one was listening.

Olive landed on the tilted deck of the Red Eyed Raven seemingly unnoticed amongst the restless spirits roaming there. The ships bell rang solemnly, the door to the below decks creaked eerily one way then the other and the tattered sails flapped on each small gasp of wind.

"Whoot hoot, this is spooky even for a night owl like me," Chloe squeaked, dodging a ghost mopping the deck.

Each transparent spirit with gaunt faces and sunken eyes was bone thin and glimmered with a blue aura. All were dressed in the tatters of what used to be sailors garments from the early nineteenth century. Ignoring the intruders, they seemed to go about their regular duties. Some swabbed decks with ghostly mops, some hoisted translucent sails, and one manned the steering wheel at what sailors call the helm, as if the ship was still under sail, even though the decks never changed from the ice-covered grave marker it was.

"That's strange. The ghosts look like they are still sailing the ship."

"They can't let go of life just because they are frozen in time, whoot hoot."

"I think we need to talk to him," Olive said looking upward.

"Who, who?" Chloe said turning her head a full one hundred and eighty degrees one way then completely around the other.

"Him."

Up on the quarterdeck stood a commanding lone spirit dressed in a dark blue overcoat with brass buttons, gold tassels on the left shoulder, and wearing a three cornered hat. With his hands clasped behind his back, he stood looking off in the distance as if the ship was at sail.

Olive floated up and landed on the quarterdeck. "Er, excuse me, sir," Olive inquired meekly.

"No one is allowed on the quarterdeck except ships officers," the raspy voice ordered with a British accent.

Olive immediately floated above the deck then asked again. "Excuse me, sir," she said as politely as she could.

"What is it? Can't you see that I am busy!" the spirit spun around showing a hideous skeletal face under a white wig. "Who are you? You are not of the ship's company."

"My name is Olive, and this is my friend, Chloe."

"How did you get on board? I gave no such permission." The ship's crew had stopped what they were doing and were now staring toward the intruders.

"We flew here. I am one of Father Christmas' reindeer," she said using the British term for Santa Claus.

"I have heard of this Father Christmas. A saint of some kind; a Yuletide elf or some such thing. He honours the Christ Child by bringing gifts to children, I believe."

"Yes, that's him. I am trying to save him."

"What brings you here on my ship? He is not here and I don't believe we have hauled any…shall we say "saint" out of the brine since we've sailed, have we, Mister Parker?"

"No, Cap'n. Not on this ship," shouted back the spirit holding on to the ship's huge steering wheel.

"Very good, Mister Parker. For a moment I thought I may have missed something."

"No, Cap'n. You don't miss much on this ship," he said, his voice tinged with the typical scorn of ship's officers.

"What is this ship, sir?" Olive asked.

"This ship is a sloop of war of the British Royal Navy named Red Eyed Raven," he answered proudly.

"Who, may I ask, is its captain?"

"That would now be me, Second Lieutenant James Squire Pittman, at your service," he said slightly doffing his cap.

"Now?"

"Yes, we were originally commanded by Captain John Edward Blizzard and our mission was to find the Northwest Passage."

"What happened to Captain Blizzard?"

The ghostly crew instantly started singing again as if the question was their cue:

Captain Blizzard became a wizard,
Stabbed the first mate in the gizzard…

Mister Parker's raspy voice rose up from where he stood at the ship's wheel and was answered deafeningly again by the rowdy crew.

Yo-ho-ho, and a bottle of rum!
Ran away like a green-eyed lizard
Off the yardarm in a blizzard
Yo-ho-ho, and a bottle of rum!

"That's enough, men," the Second Lieutenant roared. "That's the captain you're disrespecting!"

The voices died down.

"The sea can do strange things to a man," he observed with a tormented look. "The longer we got stuck in the ice the more the men went out of their minds."

"What happened, sir," Olive asked quietly.

"As the months dragged on some men ran off, only to freeze to death out there somewhere in the ice." He pointed overboard. "The fools. Others starved to death when they couldn't eat one more bite of fish." He pointed to a massive stack of fish bones at the far end of the ship.

"And your captain?"

"Our captain, well, he started reading dark passages in an unholy book he had found a long time ago, and it changed him. He became short-tempered, always moody, stayed in his cabin for days upon end ranting and raving."

Rubbing his chin, he added, "He, he turned into…well, I don't know how to say it. He became a, a monster."

"Why would he do that?"

"I don't really know. He was a good Christian man when we set sail but something soured in him. No one can reason it. It was on Christmas Day that, for no reason at all, he stabbed the first mate and ran away like a coward."

"That seems like a strange thing to do for a man in his position."

"Aye, that it does." He agreed, shaking his skull in disbelief. "He had longed to see his wife and child and constantly twirled a locket and chain containing their pictures. She had given it to him when we set sail from Portsmouth. He opened it many times during the voyage."

"He must have missed his family terribly," Olive said.

"His greatest desire was to be back in England to join them for Christmas but as our hope faded while locked in this ice, the darker his mood became. Tormented, he started saying strange things late at night, screaming at no one, talking to shadows, a man beside himself but always twirling that chain and locket. Then one day I saw that he didn't have it. I didn't think much of it until now."

"Whoot, he had issues," Chloe remarked.

"I will make a full report of his behaviour to the Admiralty when we return." He turned and looked at the crew on the lower deck. "We are all that is left of our ship's company and I am determined to get us back to England by Christmas 1814. So if you please, let me return to my duties. You are dismissed." With that Second Lieutenant Pittman turned his back and put his spyglass to his eye to resume his eternal watch, staring out to sea.

"I guess we've been dismissed." Olive said, taken aback.

"His spirit also walks this earth unsatisfied and still refuses to step through death's door, whoot hoot."

"Just like the shaman says, he has not set his mind free so that he can. In fact, none of them can," Olive said looking at the rest of the pitiable crew.

Olive floated back down to the main deck in front of a sleeveless sailor, endlessly mopping. "Excuse me sir," she said, causing him to stop his eternal swabbing.

"Aye, what can I do for ya matey," he said through a toothless grin.

"Which way would lead me to the captain's cabin?"

With a nod of his head toward the swinging door he replied, "That-a-way."

CHAPTER NINETEEN
The Captain's Cabin

To get through the door, Chloe jumped off Olive's antlers onto her back as she ducked her head and entered through the swinging door. The dank, dark corridor seemed to shrink around them. Seeping water dripped through every crack in the floor and the cobweb-laden lanterns that would have lit the way had gone out over two hundred years before.

Making her way along the murky passageway, Olive shrieked when a cobweb slithered across her face. "Eeyuk! What was that?" she cried, imagining a ghostly hand. She reared her head and an antler point stabbed the overhead beam and stuck fast. Leaping from side to side, she twisted and turned her head until it came loose.

"That could have been me! Whoot hoot!" Chloe squawked, thankful she had chosen to hop down onto Olive's back.

Another set of stairs led to the below decks and crew quarters. Olive glanced down the stairs but stayed on the captain's deck, creeping along in the darkness, her eyes wide. The tight quarters of the wooden ship made her jumpy.

"This is so spooky, whoot hoot!"

"You could say that again!"

"This is so spooky, whoot hoot!"

Tiptoeing on her delicate hooves, she finally spied a light gleaming through a crack in the door that told her she had finally reached the captain's cabin.

She nudged the door open. A blast of light reflecting off the snow streamed in through the small aft windows. Several panes of glass had been broken allowing drifts of snow to pile up on the bed and chairs. Ice covered cobwebs adorned the candelabra, maps, pen and quill, crystal wine glass, and a half-full bottle. The ship's logbooks lay strewn across the main desk and the high backed chair in the centre of the room.

"What a mess!" Olive gasped. "Where do we even start?"

"One can read a lot about a person's mind just by looking at how they keep their room, whoot hoot!"

"How are we going to find what we are looking for in this mess?" Olive lamented.

"Big meals are often made easier to digest by using one small bite at a time, whoot hoot."

Olive heard a loud cracking noise coming from the cove outside and froze. When the tremor stopped Olive said, "Chloe, hop off and search the desk. I'll look around the rest of this place."

Chloe bounced down and wobble-walked to one end of the desk and began flicking papers around with her beak.

Olive slid back the ragged curtain from around the captain's cot. She remembered the old woman saying 'you'll know it when you see it'. On the wall behind the bed hung a small shelf with a few books including a Bible. "What about his Bible?" Olive said out loud. "Grandpapa Claus really likes his."

"I think Captain Blizzard has lost heart for the word of God, which is what all his rage is about, whoot hoot."

"I guess you're right."

"Look at this box? Whoot hoot," Chloe said uncovering a tiny, ornate silver chest under one of the maps. Using her beak, she flipped the lid open. A cloud of black powder puffed out and landed all over her. "Aaaaaachoooooo! Aaaaaaachoooooo! Aaaaaaachoooooo! Whoot hoot!"

"What is it?"

"It says Saaaaaaachoooooo! Naaaaaaachoooooo! Uaaaaaaachoooooo! Faaaaaaachoooooo! And Faaaaaachoot hoot!" Chloe used her good wing to cover her nose.

"Snuff?" Olive spelled out. "It's a snuff box!"

"What is snuff? Whoot hoot!"

"Snuff is stuff people sniff to make them sneeze."

"Well…it works! Aaaaaachoooooo! Whoot hoot!"

"I don't think it's what we are looking for."

"I don't think they need to sneeze in the afterlife, or in the before life, whoot hoot!"

As Chloe spoke a spirit of one of the sailors walked through the wall carrying a ghostly tray of tea and cheese biscuits. He set it on the Captain's desk and left the room. Chloe walked through the mirage of teacup and saucer and tried to peck at the biscuits. Instead her beak tapped the wooden desk.

"I'm afraid you're not going to get to eat ghost cookies, Chloe," Olive told her, giggling.

"Don't make fun of a bird of prey with an empty stomach," Chloe said, scowling at Olive. "I have eaten large animals before you know, whoot hoot."

Surprised, Olive stared at her, wide-eyed. Then they both burst into a fit of giggles. It stopped abruptly when the ice once again shuddered under the Red Eyed Raven and sent them skidding across the icy deck.

When the ship steadied once more, Chloe stepped over to the open logbook. She couldn't read the writing but as she looked down the page, she noticed that the handwriting became messier with each daily entry until the last one. It was not much more than a splattered ink line that drifted off the page.

Olive nudged open a cabinet door with her nose and found more books, a flintlock pistol, and a naval dress sword and scabbard. There was no way she was going to take a gun or a sword to a mad man who had already stabbed the first mate and has done who-knows-what to her papa and grandpapa.

"I don't think he needs these in heaven," she mused.

On a lower shelf, a small leather satchel caught her eye. Nuzzling it with her nose she managed to open the flap to reveal thousands of beads of different colours and sizes. Some were clear like glass while others opaque; some were manmade while others were natural stone with a hole drilled through them. "Hmmm, these remind me of something I've seen before," she muttered but she couldn't put her hoof on it.

Chloe absentmindedly turned around and knocked something over with her tail feathers. It rolled off the desk and smashed on the floor. Startled, they both jumped then realized it was only the wineglass. Then Olive noticed one of Chloe's talons had caught onto one of the scattered maps and shifted it sideways. She caught a glimpse of a gold link chain.

"Is that what I think it is?" she said.

When Chloe saw it she started pecking and pulled at it like a worm from the ground, slowly revealing it from under the stack of charts and scrolls. At the other end of the chain dangled a fancy, engraved golden locket. From her clenched beak Chloe replied a muffled, "I do believe it is, whoot hoot!"

"That's it! That's what we needed to find. I can sense it." From what Second Lieutenant Pittman had told her, Olive could tell that the locket had special meaning to Captain John Edward Blizzard of the British Royal Navy.

"Whoot hoot, let's get out of here, whoot hoot!" twittered Chloe. She sensed something was about to happen as animals do prior to an earthquake.

The loud rumble in the ice was deafening and vibrated the floor once more. The ship lurched to one side sending anything not tied down sprawling to the other side of the cabin including Olive and Chloe. The wine bottle smashed to the floor, the books, maps, and scrolls slid off the table along with the candelabra, all pitching into a heap in the corner. The sword, pistol, and satchel fell out of the open cabinet and slid across the floor toward the duo along with the captain's table. Chloe, still with the locket in her beak, bounded off the desk and onto Olive's back for safety. Olive snatched the satchel from the floor and tossed it up to Chloe who seized the strap with her sharp talons.

With the ceiling too low to fly, Olive flung her head up and stabbed her antlers into the beam above, then lifted her legs just in time to let the captain's table, the sword, and the pistol slide safely under her and hit the cabin wall behind her.

The ship shook for a few moments then slowly stopped. Then seawater started to pour into the room through the broken windows in the sinking aft of the cabin.

"Oh-oh," Olive said as shook her antlers free from the beam and landed on the tilted floor.

"Abandon ship, abandon ship, all hands abandon ship, whoot hoot!" Chloe chirped, flapping her wings as the seawater streamed.

Olive crawled up the steep incline to the cabin door only to find it had shut tight during the ice break. Like she had seen Grandmama and Grandpapa do many times, she tried the door handle using her hoof on the leaver but nothing happened. She then used her teeth and pulled as hard as she could but the door still wouldn't budge.

"What do we do now?" she cried seeing the seawater rising fast. The windows of the listing ship were now completely covered with water.

Olive frantically tried the door handle again. "Please don't say this cabin will be the casket to our watery grave!" she cried.

"To Davey Jones' locker, whoot hoot!" Chloe said sadly.

Olive slumped against the cabin wall and they both watched the water slowly rise, resigning themselves to their fate. "There's nothing we can do, Chloe," Olive said.

Moments passed in silence as they helplessly watched the sea level reach Olive's hooves.

"It's been a great to meet you, Chloe. Thank-you for being my friend," Olive whimpered.

"I think the entire wheel has just fallen off our road to success, whoot hoot."

When the water reached Olive's knees she heard a scratching sound coming from the other side of the door.

"Who's there?" Olive shouted.

"It's me, Sly. I got worried about you when the ship started to sink and you didn't come back so I thought I'd better check."

"I told you to go get help at the North Pole," Olive reminded him.

"Wouldn't know how to get there and wouldn't get back in time."

"Can you help us get out of here?" Olive pleaded. "The door is stuck."

"I don't know," Sly said, frantically scratching at the door.

"Try the door handle from your side and I will try from my side. With you on the other side maybe it will give."

Sly leapt up and grabbed the leaver in his teeth and hung on using all his weight, which for an Arctic fox was not much. Olive grabbed from her side and pulled as hard as she could as the freezing water had now reached up to her belly. Sly slipped off from his grip and fell back to the floor.

"I couldn't hold on!" he yelped from the other side of the door.

"Try again Sly, the water is getting deep!"

Sly jumped up again and for a few uncertain moments, both animals strained to hold on. Then all of a sudden the door burst open sending Sly flying into the room and plunging into the water.

"Whoa, that's cold!" he screamed as he frantically splashed in the icy water, paddling toward Olive.

"Quickly, jump onto my back, we have no time." Olive yelled as the water reached her neck. Chloe moved to the top of her head and nestled between her antlers.

As he had done once before when escaping the killer whales, Sly scrambled up on Olive's back. Olive held her head low and floated out of the freezing water, through the narrow passageway, and climbed to the upper deck. Once free, she jumped over the ship's rail and galloped back to the safety of the shore.

Now away from the ship, Olive looked back and saw the ghosts going about their chores as if nothing was happening. "Don't they know their ship is sinking?"

Shivering with cold, the three friends landed safely on the shore and turned to watch the old wooden British Sloop of War, the Red Eyed Raven, slowly slip into the sea to be lost forever.

"Do you hear that?" Olive asked the others.

"Sounds like they are singing," said Sly, his teeth chattering.

"They sound happy, whoot hoot," Chloe piped with the chain and locket in her beak and the satchel in her talons.

"They are finally free and going happily to their watery graves to enter their afterlife and meet all those that went before them," Olive said shivering as ice crystallized on her fur. "I wonder if they were just waiting for us to find that locket?"

"I don't think we should hang around here any longer or we'll be meeting them as well, whoot hoot," Chloe suggested.

"You're right, Chloe. We need to get going and get Sly back home to Banks Island."

"That would be nice. I'm starting to miss my family Stone."

"Okay, all aboard." She paused, "Which way, Sly?"

"That-a-way," he said pointing his paw.

"Of course, it is," Olive said. With a smile, she lifted off and headed south.

CHAPTER TWENTY
Friends in Need

The weather had been clear and between Olive following her compass and Sly's memory for course corrections, they made it back to the rock where they had started from without any problems. It seemed like they had made it back in no time, and soon they reached Banks Island. It was time to say their final farewell to their friend.

Sly jumped off Olive's back onto the rock. "What an adventure! I'm sure going to miss you guys."

"We will miss you too, Sly," Olive said, nuzzling him with her nose. "I can't thank you enough for getting us out of that jam back on the Red Eyed Raven."

"Ditto, friend. I would have been a snack for those killer whales if it hadn't been for you two."

"I promise to come back one day and meet your family Stone."

"They will like that, especially after I tell them of our exploits. Maybe we'll meet again for more adventures."

"I think one exciting, death-defying adventure is enough for one lifetime," Olive said.

"Until we meet again, then," Sly said and scurried off.

"I'm actually going to miss him, whoot hoot."

"That's the last thing I thought you would say, Chloe, but I'll miss him, too."

The clouds started to roll in as soon as they were over the Beaufort Sea heading for the mainland. As before, Olive avoided Inuvik.

"I thought I'd take a chance and fly higher," Olive said, flying blindly through the mist of cloud. "We can use the compass to find our way, and the fishermen down there can't see us to shoot at us up here." During the flight, Chloe had hung the locket on one antler and the satchel of beads on another.

"The chance taker is the accident maker, whoot hoot!"

"How can we get into an accident up here?"

"Do you hear that? Whoot hoot."

"Hear what?"

No sooner had the words left her mouth when from out of nowhere a great commuter plane roared out of the mist toward them.

"Whoah!" Olive screamed, veering to the right to avoid a collision. She saw the eyes of the pilot widen in disbelief.

In the plane, "It can't be…" was all the stunned pilot managed to say before she heard a thump at the right rear or tail of the plane. But looking backward out of the side window she saw nothing but the heavy layer of cloud. Checking her controls she felt nothing that would force her to make an emergency landing and decided she would check the plane over when she landed in Inuvik. If there was any damage there was no way she ever going to admit she thought she saw a flying reindeer.

Olive however was not so lucky. She avoided a direct impact all right but the tail of the aircraft had clipped her left hip tearing a wide gash in her thigh. As most injured animals do when frightened, she dashed on trying to escape the scene and looking for a safe place to lick her wounds and rest.

"Whoot hoot, are you okay, Olive?" Chloe said noticing Olive had slowed down a great deal.

"I won't lie, Chloe. It really hurts," she replied after the first adrenalin rush subsided allowing her to feel the severe pain from her injury.

"We should find a place to land so you can rest, whoot hoot."

"I can't stop, Chloe. We have to push on. Grandpapa Nicholas and my papa need us."

"Better to get there late than not at all, whoot hoot."

"I know, Chloe, I know." Blood oozed from Olive's wound and her movements continued to labour as she trudged on through another snowfall. For the next several hours only her will and determination enabled her to push farther south into the tree line toward Fort Yukon.

Chloe tried to help by flapping her injured wings to give more lift but Olive gradually lost altitude. Little by little, she descended lower and lower. Her hip began to go numb and her magic dust was running out. Now, her feet clipped the tops of the trees.

Exhausted and becoming delirious, Olive knew could not go on much longer. Seeing a clearing in the trees up ahead, Olive made a valiant attempt to make it there. But she no longer had enough lift and she plowed through the fir bows that knocked her awkwardly to the snow where she tumbled and rolled to a stop in the meadow.

Dazed, Olive looked up and saw just ahead five large granite stones standing proudly right in the middle of the clearing as if put there on purpose. Knowing she could go on no longer, she thought she might find shelter from the blustery wind and snow in between the rocks. So with all the energy she could muster, she struggled to her feet. Wobbling and unsteady, she shambled toward the outcrop of granite. The wind picked up again, stirring the snow in small whirlwinds that were bitterly cold. At least they covered her tracks, she thought, as she staggered forward.

Half way there, Olive stumbled and fell to her knees. "I don't think I can make it, Chloe," she whimpered, resigned to lying out in the open for as long as it took.

"Whoot hoot, you can't give up now. Your life depends on it, whoot hoot."

"I can't go on, I'm too tired. Let me sleep," she murmured, dropping her head to the snow.

"Failure always catches up to those who lie down, whoot hoot!"

"Ooooooooooow!" The heart stopping sound from the forest ripped through them like only fear can.

"What was that?" Olive asked meekly, opening her eyes.

"I think our old enemy heard you crash in the woods, whoot hoot."

"You mean...?"

"White Storm, whoot hoot, whoot hoot."

"Oh no!" Olive's heart sank. There was no way she wanted to be caught out here in the open to face those dreadful beasts. She would be torn to pieces. Too weak to run, she dredged up the inner strength that only terror can inspire. She heaved her shattered body up and began taking small, awkward steps toward the rocks.

"Oooooooooooow!" The sound spiked her fear. They sounded even closer this time.

"We have to hide, Chloe. If they find us we're done for!" She hoped the windblown snow would cover the blood trail she was leaving behind with each step she took.

They finally reached the outcrop of rocks and squeezed between the rocks. She found a small enclave where she could lie down. Out of the wind and blinding snow, she slumped down with her last trace of energy and a deep sigh escaped her. If they were to be found now there was no way she could defend herself. She knew that White Storm and his Howling Dozen would finally have their bloodthirsty reward.

As night fell, Olive hoped that by being surrounded by the stone monuments and with the wind and snow hiding their scent, she and Chloe would remain undetected by her archenemy. At least until she got her strength back. As quietly as she could, she licked at her injured thigh hoping to make it better faster. But it was a bad gash and would take time to fully heal.

Even Chloe knew that silence was critical to their survival. She peeped not one hoot just as when hunting prey, but she knew that she and Olive were now the target. She hopped up on the rocks as high as she could to watch for White Storm, staying out of sight and camouflaged by her white feathers. She also kept a sharp eye out for the nearby hunters, allowing Olive to rest. At least she could warn her if they ever broke into the clearing.

She could hear the wolves exploring in the nearby woods where she and Olive had crashed through the tree branches. The drifting snow had covered their tracks by now. She heard them hungrily sniffing the ground at the edge of the forest, saw them search the clearing, and then head back into the woods to search some more.

In the twilight she thought she saw a faint gleam in the snow around where Olive had fallen to her knees. Chloe's golden eyes stared intently at the spot. Was there something there? But even with an owl's sharp eyesight, too much snow covered it to tell. She turned her gaze down at her friend. The compass still hung around Olive's neck and the satchel strap lay hitched over one antler but something was definitely missing. The locket was nowhere to be seen.

Chloe stretched out her injured wing, testing it. Her wing with the bullet hole was still sore and might not function like she was used to. She had to make sure she could float down to the snow. Her plan was simple: soar to where the locket lay, scoop up the chain, and get back to the top of the rock without being seen.

She waited for the moment when she thought the wolves were nowhere to be seen. In spite of intense pain, she stretched her wings and pushed off the rock and, using everything she had, she soundlessly soared over the ground toward her target. Using her good wing to manoeuvre, she angled her landing just in front of the locket.

She knew the return flight would be the most difficult. She needed to flap her injured wings to get lift. After picking up the chain with her beak, she was about to attempt it when she heard a noise at the edge of the woods. Her natural response would have been to take flight and find the highest branch for safety. Instead, Chloe froze, hoping her flecked white feathers would blend into the snow and make her invisible.

"I thought I saw something," said one of the Howling Dozen.

"What did you see?" asked White Storm.

"Something small and white moving out there in the snow."

"We are looking for a reindeer not a bunny. You know, a large deer with antlers? Did it look like that?" the leader jeered.

"Er, no."

"Then keep looking!"

Now Chloe knew she couldn't fly back. If the wolves saw her, Olive's hiding spot would be discovered. Instead, she chose the most vulnerable position a bird could take—to stay on the ground. With one small hop at a time and staying perfectly still between movements, she made sure the coast was clear before hopping again.

The young wolf vaulted out from the woods to explore again. Chloe froze while the wolf sniffed around. Chloe hoped it wouldn't catch her scent or Olive's dried blood as it crept closer and closer. Back and forth he went as though trying to zero in on a scent and came so close Chloe, standing still as a statue, that she thought he would catch her for sure. He sniffed the air, his black nostrils quivering.

He was almost upon her when out from the darkness yelled the familiar raspy angry voice, "What did I tell you, fool! Get back here and look for the reindeer and forget the bunnies!" The young wolf's shadow loomed over Chloe as she held her breath. Then he lifted his head, turned, and ran back to the forest.

With her heart racing, Chloe gasped at her good fortune. Once again she began creeping back to the rocks until, with great relief, she reached the gap and crawled into the hiding place. She placed the chain and locket back over the sleeping Olive's antlers without disturbing her. Then, exhausted, she curled up in the curve of Olive's body and closed her eyes.

"Well, well, what do we have here?" snarled White Storm as he stood on the rock overlooking Olive's and Chloe's resting place.

Olive woke with a start and looked up in terror at the white wolf standing over them, bathed in the light of the morning sun. Still sore and unable to move, she cast about for a way out and instead saw the Howling Dozen on every ledge and in every gap surrounding them. To escape, Chloe jumped up onto another rock only to come face-to-face with the snarl of the young wolf that had stood over her the evening before. Reluctantly, she hopped back down to be with Olive.

"Finally, I have you," sneered White Storm, "and you won't escape me this time."

"But…" was all Olive managed to squeak.

"You will make the most wonderful of suppers for me and my Howling Dozen!" he growled as the rest of the snickering pack cackled with glee. "Or should I say, breakfast?" he said to another roar of howling laughter.

"But, but you can't!" pleaded Olive.

"Why not? You will be so tasty and our bellies are empty from searching for you all night."

"I have to save Santa!" she implored.

"Who is this Santa? He means nothing to me," White Storm replied. "Get 'em boys," he ordered.

The wolves edged in for the kill and were about to pounce when one of them suddenly yelped. Olive heard the crack of a rifle.

"What was that?" howled White Storm.

"Hunters!" yelled one of the pack.

Another bullet zinged off the stone where White Storm stood, sending him tumbling off the rock. Several more cracks from the rifle sent all the wolves scattering for cover. The pack hauled their injured companion into the safety of the woods by the scruff of his neck. Bullets whizzed, chasing the Howling Dozen into the dark forest shadows at top speed.

White Storm stopped his retreat, stood on a fallen tree and howled in anguish. "Not again! Owoooooooooo!"

Chloe jumped up higher on the rock to see who was shooting, careful not to be seen.

"Who is it, Chloe?" asked Olive in a faint voice.

"Whoot hoot, it's the humankind child with Rusty, Dusty, and the rest of the dog team!" Chloe cried as the sled team approached.

"Akliak! Awesome! Try to get his attention," Olive pleaded.

Chloe jumped up and down flapping her wings and hooting until she saw the dog team and sled turn in their direction.

"Whoot hoot, they've seen me, they've seen me. Whoot hoot!"

Akliak pulled up the sled at the narrow entrance in the rocky outcrop. "Whoa, fellas, whoa," he called, stepping hard on the sled's brake. The huskies yipped and yelped, prancing around in the snow. "Stay!" Akliak commanded the team. He jumped off the sled and crawled between the rocks to find Olive, lying injured in the snow with a familiar compass around her neck and a locket and satchel hanging from her antlers.

"What happened to you, little reindeer?" he asked.

Olive lifted her pleading brown eyes, then started licking her wound again.

"You've been hurt," he said. "I bet those nasty wolves did this to you. Wait here." He shouldered his rifle and went back to the sled. When he returned he carried a dressing, bandage, and some tape from his first aid kit and attended the wound.

"Now, let's get you out of here and back to Grandmother. She will know how to help you." Akliak helped Olive stand then walked her to the narrow gap, letting her lean on him as they squeezed through. Chloe jumped onto her back and they made their way out to the dogsled.

"Yup, yup, yup, Olive, Olive, Olive," yelped Dusty, wagging his tail so hard it spun him around.

"Uh huh, uh huh, got hurt, got hurt, got hurt," said Rusty, sniffing at the dressing on the wound.

To Akliak, the dogs' whimpering made no sense. "You lie down in the sled," he said, gently helping Olive onto the fur rug, "and we will get you back to Fort Yukon."

Akliak covered her with the hide of a caribou to keep her warm, and Olive shuddered and choked at the smell. Chloe jumped up to ride on to the handle bar of the sled and Akliak yelled, "Mush!"

As they made their way through the trails with the dogs pulling and riding on the sled skids, Akliak began asking questions. "Were you out here all this time? Was it scary out here all alone? Why didn't you just fly yourself out of trouble?"

Olive remained silent.

"Maybe I was wrong. Maybe you can't fly," Akliak pondered out loud.

Olive closed her eyes and fell sound asleep for the rest of the journey. She woke when she heard the dogs yelping

"Yup, yup, yup we're here, we're here, we're here," said Dusty.

"Uh huh, Uh, huh, here, here, here," said Rusty along with the chorus from the rest of the dog team.

They pulled up in front of the Gwitch'in elder, Alice's house, without anywhere near the fanfare of the first time. Akliak called out, "Grandmother, come quick! Look what I found out in the wilderness and brought back home."

"What is all the fuss about?" Alice enquired opening her door with an apron on and her hands covered in flour. "I was baking cookies."

"Sorry, Grandmother, but look." Akliak pulled back the hide to reveal a sleepy Olive looking up at her.

"Oh, my goodness! Olive!" Alice said, rushing down the porch steps with arms open to hug her. Then she saw the bandage and cried, "You've been hurt!"

"The wolves had her trapped up at the ceremony rocks," Akliak explained.

"Oh dear!"

"I scared them away, see?" he said, showing her the rifle that he had lost before.

"It's good that you found it, Akliak, or Olive here might not have survived those zhoh. Help me bring her in where it's warm."

With the help of Alice and Akliak, Olive stood and the trio made their way up the porch stairs. Chloe hopped in behind and managed to flutter up to the stair railing then followed her friend into the house.

Once Olive had been settled in front of the fire, Alice took off the bandage to reveal the nasty wound. She could see that it was no bite wound.

"Thank you, Akliak, for saving the Vadzaih. You did the right thing bringing her back here."

"I'm glad, Grandmother. I couldn't let those wolves slaughter one of Santa's Reindeer." He watched his Grandmother's face for any clue that this might be the truth but received only a deliberate stare in return. "I know, I know," he sighed. "Go see to the dogs. Make sure they are fed and kennelled."

"That's a very good idea, grandson."

"I know that reindeer can fly," he hollered as he went out the door. "You can't fool me. I just know it!"

"Now tell me what happened little one," Alice asked after he had closed the door. As she cleaned the wound and got out a needle and thread to stitch up the gash, Olive told her about the long journey back to Banks Island, how Sly had helped them find the Red Eyed Raven, and about the ghosts they found.

"That must have been difficult for you," Alice said softly.

"The best way out of difficulty is through it, whoot hoot!"

"So true, Chloe," Alice replied.

Olive shared how they had found the chain and locket and narrowly escaped the captain's cabin when the ship began to sink. She told the old lady how after saying goodbye to Sly, the aeroplane had come out of the clouds had struck her.

"I didn't think that gash you have was made by wolves," Alice reasoned. "That must have been frightening for you." She dabbed healing ointment on the wound then placed a new bandage over it.

"Not as scary as White Storm, whoot hoot!"

"I can imagine."

"When I couldn't go on any farther, we crash-landed in the woods. We hoped the wolves wouldn't find us if we hid between the boulders in the clearing but somehow they did. We had no way out and if it hadn't been for Akliak coming along just in time, we would be goners by now. You must find a way to thank him for us."

"I will but remember, you saved him and I will forever be thankful to you."

Olive gave her a tiny smile. "We brought something for you, Grandmother."

"And what would you two bring an old woman like me?"

"The satchel on my antlers," Olive told her, tilting her head.

Alice retrieved the satchel and opened it to find all the original nineteenth century beads. "Oh, my goodness! These are like our ancestral beads made from real stones and porcelain!" She held up one to the light. "Oh, Olive, they are beautiful!"

"I saw them in the captain's cabin and remembered that you wore a vest with beads when I met you. I thought you might like them. It was the least we could do to thank you for helping Chloe."

"I love them! Thank you! I see you also brought back a locket on a chain," Alice said.

"The ghost in charge of the ship, a seaman named Second Lieutenant James Squire Pittman, said it was a favorite of Captain Blizzard. His wife had given it to him on the very day they set sail on their voyage."

Alice lifted the chain from Olive's antlers and opened the locket to reveal the tiny paintings of Captain Blizzard's wife and son. "I think this will work," she mused. "Now you rest because we have a long journey in front of us."

We? Olive thought, but was too tired to pursue it further.

CHAPTER TWENTY-ONE
Jenny's Mystery

After another twenty-four hours of deep slumber, Olive woke feeling a lot better even though her hip ached. Groggy from almost too much sleep, she asked, "How long have I been out?"

"Almost thirty-six hours, little one. You mumbled in your sleep and had a bit of fever but it broke during the night," the shaman explained.

Olive was unaware that while she had been sleeping, Alice had stood watch over her. She had applied cool compresses to keep her temperature down, changed the bandages, and made sure the stitches were holding the wound together. She had applied ointment to soothe the soreness and keep the infection away. Even Chloe had benefitted from the extra attention to her wing. Her flight feathers were already starting to come in and cover the bullet hole.

"Oh wow, we have to get going," Olive said trying to stand only to wobble and collapse back down.

"Not so fast, Olive. You've had quite a trying time and need more rest. I have made a broth with some herbs and berries to help you heal faster. You need food to get your strength back."

But Olive felt the uncontrollable urge to leave and was restless to continue her journey. "I cannot," she said. "It really is time for us to go. Grandpapa Nick and the reindeer need our help."

"But you can't even stand, let alone fly."

Olive tried to stand again only to feel her knees buckle once more. Alice was right; she definitely needed more rest. "But…" was all she managed to say.

Alice sighed. "If you insist, give me a minute to pack a couple of things and we'll get going. Eat the broth I've made while you wait, the both of you. You must have something to eat or you'll never be able to face the wizard."

"You do know owls don't eat soup, whoot hoot."

"You do today, young lady," the old woman ordered on her way out the door. "Now eat!"

While a reluctant Chloe made strange faces, Olive ate the delicious broth and minutes later, Alice pulled up outside the house with her pickup truck. She came back in to help Olive get up and limp to the rear of the truck where she had laid a board down from the tailgate as a ramp.

"What are you doing, Grandmother?" Olive asked.

"I knew you wouldn't be able to fly for several days when I saw you come in as sick as you were. That's why I knew I had to come with you. This way you can rest until we get to Denali. And Akliak and the other suspicious eyes around here might change their minds as to who they think you really are if they see you lying in the back of my pickup truck."

"I guess so," Olive managed to groan as she lay down stiffly on the soft straw bed Alice had prepared for her.

Chloe hopped up onto the window ledge that was open between the cab and the truck bed.

Under the watchful and disbelieving eyes of Akliak and some of the neighbours, Alice pulled away from the house with her new passengers on board. She headed straight toward the Fort Yukon airport.

The cold, crisp morning air was refreshing but the potholes in the ice-covered road let Olive know with each jarring bump that the wound she was nursing was still a long way from being healed. Though her energy was slowly returning, she knew she wasn't ready to fly.

When they arrived at the airport, Olive grew anxious and agitated. She'd already had one bad experience with aircraft.

"Oh, don't be worried, Olive," Alice assured her. "It will be okay."

"You didn't say anything about an aeroplane!" Olive said, struggling to her feet. To her, flying injured would be far better than getting into a machine like the one she had seen strewn all over the ground farther north.

"I know you were hit by one but aeroplanes are really quite safe," Alice told her before heading toward an area near the hangers.

"Not from what we saw, whoot hoot," Chloe chirped, equally worried. "We saw the wreckage of an airplane scattered all over an island."

"But there is no road to Fairbanks at this time of year. It's the only way to get there."

"I think I'd rather fly myself and take my chances," Olive said, standing unsteadily in the back of the pickup.

The old woman put her forehead to Olive's and whispered, "There is no way I'd let anyone or anything hurt you. You have to trust me. You will need every ounce of your strength when you have to face the Blizzard Wizard, believe me."

"Okay, I guess…" she replied, still uneasy.

"You may as well go with it, Olive," Chloe chimed in. "She is like a baseball umpire; she will never reverse her decision! Whoot hoot."

Alice pulled down the ramp and led Olive from the truck bed. "I have a friend who will sneak us all onto her cargo plane. She's heading back to Fairbanks empty. Aren't we lucky?"

"A true friend is one who flies in when the rest fly out, whoot hoot!"

Alice led them out to the tarmac and as soon as Olive saw the aircraft she bucked and wanted to run.

"What's the matter, dear?" Alice asked, grabbing the compass' leather strap that hung around Olive's neck.

"That's the plane that hit us!" Olive cried.

"It is? Oh my," Alice said in the most calming voice she could muster. "Don't be nervous. I'll be right there with you, dear. Every step of the way."

"Never call a restless reindeer nervous. She may be wearing itchy underwear! Whoot hoot," Chloe joked, attempting to break the tension.

They saw a woman in a parka striding toward them. "Now, hush little ones," Alice said, "here comes the pilot."

"I recognize this reindeer!" the pilot said excitedly. "You can fly!"

"Well, that's the end of that secret. Whoot hoot," Chloe said quietly enough so only Alice and Olive could hear her.

"Oh Jenny, my dear, you must be mistaken. My Grandson found this reindeer out in the wild after wolves attacked her. He brought her back in his dog sled," Alice explained.

"It sure looks like the reindeer I saw when I was flying supplies up to Inuvik, Grandmother," she said respectfully. "I am pretty sure she had an owl with her as well. In fact, the thing hit my plane, I'm sure of it, and if I were to guess, right around where this reindeer looks injured." Jenny looked suspiciously at the bandage on Olive's left hip.

"I'm just taking her to the Fairbanks vet to get some better treatment on her thigh and the owl is my friend. I call her Chloe," Alice said then leaned closer. "Are you saying you saw a flying reindeer while you were flying? You don't want that idea to get around."

"I, I, thought I did," the pilot stuttered. "Maybe my eyes were playing tricks on me that day," she said, but Alice could tell she was still unconvinced.

"Jenny, why would I need a flight to Fairbanks if this reindeer could fly?"

"I guess you're right," Jenny said. "Let's get her on board. I have to be in the air in five minutes."

Alice whispered to Olive, "Now, don't you worry, little one. It takes less than an hour through the White Mountains to get to Fairbanks, so please try to relax. I'll be right here beside you."

Everything in Olive was on high alert and she fought every natural instinct to run as she was led into the cargo hold of the aircraft. The feel of metal beneath her hooves and the smell of oil and fuel made her twitch with uncertainty. Her heart pounded. After the doors closed, she lay down on some blankets laid out for her, with Chloe perched in her familiar spot. Alice sat comfortingly on the floor next to her and drew Olive's head onto her lap.

The aircraft shuddered and roared to life when the engines fired and the whining propellers started to turn. Olive jumped when Jenny released the brakes and the plane began to taxi toward the runway while Chloe flapped her wings and squawked in futile protest.

"It's okay, you two," Alice said, her voice calm while she gently rubbed Olive's face. "I know you're scared but everything is okay. I'm right here," she assured them.

The plane roared down the runway and finally lifted its nose up into the air and within moments they were off heading south to Fairbanks. Olive and Chloe only began to relax when the aircraft levelled out and they got used to the drone of the engines.

With Cashe Mountain the highest peak at nearly five thousand feet, and the Rosebud Summit nearly four thousand, Jenny flew as low as she could between peaks and through the valleys with the heaters on full blast to keep her passengers warm. The sun beamed in through the small windows. Over the noise of the aeroplane, she yelled to her passengers, "We are lucky today, there's a report of heavy dark clouds with lightning around Mount Denali but we should be okay with clear skies until we get to Fairbanks."

"That's great," Alice replied knowing full well who might be the cause of the storm over Denali. She fretted over the conflict she knew Olive would face and gave her another calming pat as the small reindeer slept. Alice knew there was no point in upsetting her now; the challenge of Olive's life would be soon upon her.

With only a couple of bumps of turbulence, they descended, then felt the wheels of the cargo plane thumping down at Fairbanks Airport. The engines roared as the plane slowed down. Jenny taxied the plane to the cargo area and brought it to a stop.

Once she saw that the area was clear of any witnesses, Jenny opened up the cargo doors and let the fresh air in. The relieved hitchhikers stumbled out. "Thank you so much, Jenny. I owe you one," Alice said gratefully, squeezing the pilot's arm.

"No problem, Grandmother. Anything for our elders." She also was a member of the Gwitch'in people. "Is there anything else I can do?"

"You've been such a great help that I hate to ask but do you think you could stay here with Olive until I get back? I have to rent a pickup truck."

"No worries, Grandmother. I have to secure the aircraft anyway." After Alice had gone out of sight she couldn't resist asking, "So your name is Olive, is it? Did Grandmother give that to you name or did Santa Claus?"

Olive wanted to say her name was given to her by her papa, Prancer, but instead remained quiet and stared mutely at the pilot. Having one of the humankind know her identity was quite enough if the secret were to stay secret. It was obvious to Olive that no matter what story Alice had told her, Jenny would still be convinced that Olive was the flying reindeer that she nearly ran into while flying to Inuvik.

"So you're not talking, eh?" she said, shaking her head.

Awkward moments passed under Jenny's watchful eye. Olive pretended not to notice and Chloe pretended to sleep until Alice finally pulled around the corner driving a brand new Ford pickup truck with a rental sticker in the back window.

After laying the blankets down in the back and finding another board for a ramp, Alice led Olive, still limping, up into the bed and settled her down for the four-hour journey to the Denali State Park.

"Are you sure Olive isn't one of Santa's reindeer?" Jenny persisted as she helped Alice with the ramp.

"I only know of Dasher, Dancer, Prancer, Vixen, Comet, Cupid, Donner, Blitzen and, of course, Rudolf," Alice replied. "Never an Olive."

"I guess you're right, Grandmother," Jenny said with a shrug and a sigh.

When Olive slumped down in the back of the truck she cheekily gave Jenny a wink. Jenny did a double take then shook her head as Alice pulled out, heading for the Parks Highway.

"I knew it!" was all Alice could hear as she pulled away.

CHAPTER TWENTY-TWO
Off to See the Wizard

Alice pulled out of the airport and along the snow-cleared Airport Way to Highway 3 and took the ramp heading northwest. It didn't take long before the Parks Highway curved southward and they were on their way to Denali.

As they travelled along the snow-banked highway, Olive soon got used to the disbelieving stares she got from drivers as other vehicles passed by. But with brisk air whipping around the truck bed, she eventually put her head down to rest. She realized in this position she looked more like a hunting trophy than a live reindeer. Chloe was more comfortable perched in her spot in the back window to watch where they were headed.

They passed Skinny Dick's Halfway Inn, over Little Goldstream Creek, Parks Highway Service and Towing, Jeep Trail intersection, and followed alongside before crossing over the Tanana River without any incident.

"Keep your head down, Olive," Alice called through the open window. "We are coming into Nenana. I'm going to stop for gas so pretend you are dead."

"Dead?"

"Yes, that way everyone will think I've been hunting and won't bother us. If they see that you are alive, they will only start asking questions."

"Olive, you can live through almost anything except death but now you can survive pretending to die, whoot hoot!"

She flopped her head back down and closed her eyes.

When Alice pulled out from the station, she saw the State Trooper patrol car parked at the Trail Break Coffee house but thought nothing of it. She continued on past the Nenana Court House, the Airport Road intersection, and past the Cemetery Road turn off. It was only when she passed the FAA Way T-junction that she saw the blue lights flashing behind her.

Alice pulled over to the edge of the snow-covered road. *What have I done now? I don't think I was speeding*, she thought. As the officer approached the passenger side with his right hand over his holster, she rolled her window down and kept her hands on the wheel. State Troopers were notoriously nervous approaching strange vehicles at traffic stops.

"Driver's Licence and Registration please, ma'am."

Alice dug her licence out of her purse, plus the rental agreement insurance and handed them over to the officer.

"Do you know why I am pulling you over, ma'am?"

"Actually, I don't, young man," she replied politely.

"You have a reindeer in the back of your truck and I don't see a hunting tag. Do you have a license with you, ma'am?"

"Yes I have, and no I haven't, but her name is Olive."

"Olive? Do you always name your kills?" He craned his neck and looked in the back, then noticed the bandage on Olive's hip.

"Well, of course not, officer," Alice replied. "Olive is alive."

"Alive! It looks quite dead to me," he said lifting one of Olive's antlers. Trying not to react, Olive lay still.

"Oh, I assure you she is quite alive," Alice said. "Olive, you can look up now. This nice officer doesn't believe you are alive."

Olive popped her head up and the State Trooper stumbled backwards. "Why would you have a live reindeer in the back of your truck?" he spluttered, eyes wide. "And, and…how does this, this reindeer understand you?"

"It is such a long story but as you can see, she has been injured and I am helping her get to Denali," she said truthfully.

Shaking his head, the officer looked at the bandage on Olive's hip and then noticed the locket on her antlers and a compass hanging around her neck, "Why the compass?"

"It's so she can find her way of course?" Alice answered, pasting an expression of innocence on her face.

"Ma'am," he said sternly, "why on earth would a reindeer need a compass?" he said ignoring the locket.

"Simple. She gets lost without it."

"Ahhhgh!" The officer shook his head in frustration. "I'll be right back." He strode back to his patrol car to check Alice's Drivers' License, still shaking his head. "Why always me?" he muttered.

A few minutes later he came back. "Well ma'am, everything checks out and you are free to go but I still have to ask the big question. Why do you have a live reindeer sitting in the back of your pickup truck?"

"Do you really want to know?" Alice took her papers from his hand. "You won't believe me if I told you."

"Ma'am, I've heard all the stories you can imagine on these highways and nothing can shock me anymore."

"I'm sure this one will," she continued. "This reindeer is the daughter of Prancer, you know, one of Santa's reindeer? And she has been sent out to find Santa by Mrs. Claus because he's been missing since Christmas Eve. I'm giving her a lift to Mount Denali to face the Blizzard Wizard. Got it?"

"Uh...huh..." The officer's mouth hung open in disbelief as he watched Alice pull away. Looking in the rear-view mirror she saw him growing fainter, with his hands on his hips and his head shaking.

"Well, he's got a story the gang tonight," she giggled knowing he probably thought her a crazy old lady.

As she travelled farther south, the weather started to close in. Dark clouds gathered and wet snowflakes dotted the windshield. They crossed Fish Creek for the first time. Snow-covered trees, half-buried reflectors on tall rods to denote the road edges, and telephone poles slid by with mesmerizing regularity.

Time ticked by slowly as they sped along the desolate highway following the ruts left by other vehicles. It had been a while since the plow had gone through but at least the road was open. After losing radio reception a while back and with no CDs in the rental truck, Alice started to sing to pass the time. With one of Santa's reindeer in the back it wasn't hard to start humming some of the Christmas favourites. Christmas was over by now but January sixth was just around the corner signifying Christmas for those of Orthodox Christian faith.

They crossed Fish Creek a second time, passed the Fireweed Roadhouse, a few lakes, and more trees. Next came Julius Creek, the Clear Airport, Radio Tower Road, and over the Nenana River that was frozen and covered with snow. Finally they drove over the Healy River and through the town of Healy, giving Alice the landmark she needed. "Not too long now, Olive," she shouted through the back window. "The next stop is Denali."

"A town so small even the roosters sleep in until noon! Whoot hoot."

"Oh, stop it, Chloe," Alice retorted. "There are lots of small towns and villages in Alaska with really nice people who get up before dawn to go to work."

"No dream comes true until you wake up and go to work, whoot hoot!"

Olive was now feeling better. The rest had given her more energy. She knew she was going to need all she could get to be ready to face the wizard. She still had no idea how she was going to defeat the wizard and hoped Chloe would come along with her, though she certainly didn't have to.

They crossed into McKinley Park, past the Denali Airport, and a little farther on, Alice finally pulled off the highway at the Veteran's Memorial. It was closed for the winter. "Well, Olive, we're finally here," she said plowing the truck through the deep snow before stopping in the empty parking lot and getting out.

Standing proudly, she noticed the five snow-covered columns with star-shaped openings honouring all the veterans from the different military services, including the coast guard. In a moment of respect, Alice stood speechless and in awe feeling a shiver come over her not from the cold, but from what the monuments commemorating the heroic lives lost serving people.

Olive hopped down from the pickup and looked up to the ominous clouds that surrounded the top of Mount Denali off in the distance. The sky rumbled with thunder and blue forks of lightning zigzagged out of the blackest of the hanging clouds, lighting up the face of Denali. It looked unnatural and eerie. "The wizard appears angry," Alice observed.

"Those at war with others are seldom at peace with themselves, whoot hoot!"

"So true, Chloe. Are you sure you want to do this, Olive?" Alice asked, placing a hand on Olive's neck just behind her antlers and giving her a pat.

"I must, Grandmother. If Santa and my papa are up there somewhere, I must try to save them."

"I will be here for you and pray for your safe return," the grandmother said.

"Thank-you, but you don't have to. I will either save them or meet the same fate."

"We will see about that," she said.

"I'm coming with you. Whoot hoot!"

"Chloe, you are my best friend and I appreciate your offer but I wouldn't want to put you in danger. Why not stay with Grandmother until you are completely healed, and then go back home?"

"What kind of friend would I be? I may not be able to fly but I have a sharp beak and a nice set of talons, whoot hoot." She bravely stretched out her impressive claws.

"Are you sure, Chloe? This will be so dangerous."

"Dangerous for him! Whoot hoot!" she squawked with attitude and bravely hopped onto Olive's antlers.

"Thank-you, my friend," Olive said, relieved she wouldn't have to go alone. The she floated into the air and began her drift toward the mountain.

"Good luck, Olive, and you too, Chloe," Alice called after them.

It felt good to be flying again as she stretched her legs and started up the Coffee River Valley toward Moose's Tooth and Bear's Tooth Mountains. The low mountains on each side looked beautiful covered in deep snow and the Coffee River widened to look like a long frozen lake rather than a river. The farther she went through the channel, the more the pass narrowed making her feel as though she were being led down a path to a dark destiny.

"Chloe, I don't like the looks of this," Olive said feeling the unease creep over her at every turn.

"Whoot hoot, there are no detours along the straight and narrow path!"

"I know, Chloe, but my knees are shaking."

"The highway of fear is the shortest route to defeat, whoot hoot!"

When she reached Moose's Tooth she could see the Denali Mountain ahead. Black clouds surrounded its peak shooting out lightning shards of blue energy in every direction. Olive shuddered at the prospect of having to go up there to find the wizard's cave but she pressed on, determined.

She flew through the valley next to Rooster Comb Mountain and Mount Kulich and made the final turn toward the tallest mountain. She started her climb up the cliff face of Mount Denali with the East Buttress on her right. It wasn't long before the wind and snow became blinding and swirled ferociously about her as she ascended the rocky crags.

"I can't see where I'm going!" she cried, wincing as ice crystals pelted down upon them in the same way they had in the arctic.

"Determination is always daring your heart to go farther than what you can see, whoot hoot!"

The higher up she went, the stronger the winds blew, bowling her backwards several times. After each time she got back upright and doggedly carried on. She could feel the magic draining rapidly in her effort to make the climb and hoped she would have enough left once they reached the top.

Chloe gripped the locket with her talons so as not to lose it in this terrible storm. Looking down into the purple abyss she knew losing it now would mean it would be lost forever. No one would ever find it again on this mountain.

Several times Olive used the rocks as a shield to catch her breath from the wind and bitter bite of the crystallized snow relentlessly and violently bombarding them. The higher she went, the less oxygen filled her lungs making the gruelling climb even tougher. At each stop she was forced to rest longer.

After finding shelter behind a crag, she said, "I don't think I have enough magic to make it, Chloe." Her breath came in great gulps.

"Negative thinkers always put on the brakes while positive thinkers don't have any, whoot hoot!"

"Okay, okay, I get it. Let's keep going," she said, turning back into the wind.

Olive continued up the mountain moving from one rock to another, fighting the blizzard the wizard was continuing to summon with his outstretched staff. Then, while resting between two hulking boulders she heard a muffled rumble over the howling wind, a sound she hadn't heard before. "What was that?" she cried feeling the rumble ripple through her body.

Looking up, all she could see was pelting ice and darkness but the clamour grew louder and louder. "Whoot hoot, whoot hoot, move! Move!" Chloe shrieked over the deafening noise. She had seen one of these before.

"But..."

"Whoot hoot, move! Move! Move now!"

Without a word, Olive dashed for cover behind another rock, reaching it just in time before an avalanche roared past like a freight train, around and over them all at once.

Huddling as low and as tightly to the face of the granite block as they could possibly cling, they both squeezed their eyes shut and prayed the stone would hold and not be sent tumbling down the mountainside, taking them with it along with ice and other debris.

The white blanket recklessly crashed past them, bellowing loud with the resentment of having to hastily shift. Finally, the ocean of snow exhausted its energy and became still once again as if nothing had happened.

"Wow, that was close! Are you all right, Chloe," Olive enquired when the rumbling finally subsided.

"My feathers are a little ruffled but I think I'm okay, whoot hoot!"

Olive peered out from behind the rock to see what caused the avalanche. Looking upward she saw a dark hooded figure, standing with his legs spread on a flat rocky outcrop. Under the glow of never-ending lightning bolts, the menacing figure stood insanely roaring in hysterical laughter, in his outstretched arm he held a staff that discharged mighty zaps of electric blue energy.

"Well, I think we've found the culprit," Olive said.

CHAPTER TWENTY-THREE
The Blizzard Wizard

In the flashing light display going on and off as if a child were playing with a light switch, Olive could now see the wild eyes of the Blizzard Wizard glaring off into the distance with all the hatred of a demon held in the endless torment of hell. For a moment the flashes reminded Olive of when the elves put a flashlight under their chin to make scary faces at Halloween. But this one was no joke; it was as real as it ever gets.

"He certainly looks angry," she said, gazing up at the figure.

"Anger is just one letter short of danger! Whoot hoot!"

"We are going to have to be very careful," Olive advised.

With only a short distance between the wizard and Olive, she noticed behind him the dark entrance to a cave. Covered with icicles it looked like the cavernous mouth of a great white shark.

"Whoa, scary!" Olive cried. "I wonder if Santa, Papa, and the other reindeer are being kept down in there?"

"Humankind always keep their most prized possessions close to them, whoot hoot!"

"I have to find out."

"I don't recommend knocking on his door. He might answer, whoot hoot!"

"Maybe there is another way."

Hoping the wizard's snowstorm would prevent her from being seen, Olive tiptoed out from her hiding spot, planning to sneak behind him unnoticed between flashes. She moved from one boulder to another in complete darkness. Then she stepped on some loose shale and sent a small avalanche of snow and rock sliding down the mountain. She held her breath.

"Who dares stand on my mountain!" thundered the wizard, Captain John Edward Blizzard. Pointing his magic staff he cast another crackling lightning bolt toward the slipping rocks.

Olive ducked behind the nearest rock. The bolt hit the boulder and wrapped it in solid ice. It took several long seconds for her heart to slow down then, hoping he had not seen her, she poked her nose out once more.

"This is going to be more difficult than I imagined," she whispered to Chloe.

When nothing more moved, the Blizzard Wizard went back to conjuring his angry tempest spells and laughing hideously in its pure evil pleasure.

Olive saw another break and decided to try to reach the entrance to the cave again but this time she floated just above the ground so as to not loosen any more rocks. She made another dash for cover but the wizard must have seen her. He spun toward her and sent another bolt of lightning in her direction.

"Whoot hoot, jump!" Chloe shrieked to the stunned Olive.

Olive reacted, leaping straight up in the air in time to see the ice bolt pass under her and hit another snow-covered granite monument.

"I know someone is there. Show yourself!" commanded the Blizzard Wizard, peering through the night of whirling snow.

By bounding up into the night sky and with the wizard seeming to be unaware of the existence of any more flying reindeer, Olive avoided detection in the bleak darkness. But the unexpected raging wind blew her sideways toward the glacier and worst of all, no cover.

Using the skills she had learned when she flew into the storm while crossing through the enchanted curtain, Olive corrected her spin and turned into the wind to stabilize. "Spread your wings," she called to Chloe. Once upright, and with Chloe clinging desperately to her antlers, she used her body and Chloe's wings like a sailboat and tacked her way toward the walls of the glacier where the wind was not so fierce.

It was risky to hide between the cracks of glacial ice caused by the previous avalanche. Another slab could break away at any moment and careen down the mountain, but to get close to the cave it was a risk she had to take. When she saw the break between lightning bolts she dashed down into one of the crevasses and hid against a wall of sheer ice.

"Whew, we made it, Chloe," Olive said, panting. "He can't see us in here."

Cracking and moaning sounds echoed through the chasm as the ice walls moved slowly down the mountain. Olive and Chloe both flinched at the slightest noise the glacier made as if it protested having intruders in its crevasses.

"We can't stay in here long, Chloe. This thing might give way at any moment," Olive said cautiously.

"We become either crushed ice or ice cubes, whoot hoot!"

"Well, hopefully neither." Olive poked her head out to see if the wizard was still looking in their direction. From her position she could see where the wind had blown them so they were now off to one side of the wizard and much nearer the cave entrance.

"We may be in luck, Chloe. From here we may be able to sneak up behind him unseen," she said eagerly.

Using the ridges of the glacial face, Olive crept on nimble hooves toward the rocky outcrop with the mysterious cave and its miserable guardian, the Blizzard Wizard. Hiding behind a crag, she saw that she was now closer than what she had been before. If she were to glide past the wizard, her timing would have to be perfect.

"I will wait until he casts another thunder and lightning spell so he won't hear me slip into the cave."

"But you will be in the light, whoot hoot!"

"I have to take that chance. Hopefully he will be too busy making blizzards to notice me!"

She took her time, watching the Blizzard Wizard raise his arms several times, pointing his staff toward the rumbling dark sky. He closed his eyes each time he spoke a summoning spell, and they would snap open as he watched each violent, blue bolt shoot from the tip of his staff. Then his dreadful laugh pierced the air as the bolt shot deep into the clouds above to light up the night sky.

At the moment the thunder cracked its loudest, Olive slipped silently into the cave. Her simple plan had worked. Hugging the walls of ice she crept through the darkness, deeper into the cavern with only the echo from drips of slowly melting ice to mask her frightened panting. Before long she sensed another large opening and stopped.

When the next flash of lightning filled the room with light, Olive finally saw what had happened to Grandpapa Nick, her papa, and the rest of the reindeer. Astonished, she gasped in horror. "Grandpapa!" she cried.

There before her, frozen in solid ice like a tapestry hanging on the wall and captured in mid-flight, was the blurry, blue image of Santa sitting in his sleigh with the reins still clasped in his hands. In front of him were the nine reindeer including her papa, Prancer, frozen in place. They looked exactly like the pictures one sees on a Christmas card.

At the next flash she saw the ice cave with its frosted desk and chair, a lantern, and a few relics so old that they were unrecognizable. The following flash revealed the thick ice Santa and the team were fixed behind. "Oh, my goodness! How am I going to get you out of there?" she cried, hardly believing what she saw.

"Is that you, Olive?" She was sure she'd heard a muffled voice from the ice.

"Yes it's me, Grandpapa. I'm here to rescue you!"

"Thank goodness, little one. I thought we were lost forever."

"How do I get you out of there, Grandpapa?"

"I really don't know but we cannot help you. We can't move at all."

"Doing beats stewing, whoot hoot!" Chloe commented.

"You're right, Chloe. We've got to do something." Olive backed up as far as the cave would allow. "Now hop off, Chloe. I don't want you to get hurt."

Chloe fluttered up to a ledge, well out of the way.

With all the force she could muster, Olive rammed the ice wall with her antlers only to stagger back having chipped out only a few chunks of ice.

"Well, that's one way to break the ice! Whoot hoot!" Chloe said.

"Whoa, that's hard!" Olive said, shaking her head.

At the next flash and clap of thunder Olive rammed the ice wall again breaking more chips off but it was obvious she would have to be here a long time before she would be able to break the wall down completely.

Again and again she butted the ice, timing her attacks, but with not much success other than the start of a headache. Finally, she was able to chip the ice away around Santa's face. "Good girl, Olive," Santa said, relieved. "Now if you can free my hand I might be able to reach my magic dust." Just as the words left his mouth the room lit up with an eerie cobalt glow.

Olive sucked in a gasp of fear. She turned slowly around to see the Blizzard Wizard standing ominously in the cave entrance. His black-cloaked outline glowed from the ever-present lightning flashes behind him.

"What do we have here? Another flying reindeer?" He screamed and pointed his staff at Olive freezing her instantly with a bolt of solid ice.

"Noooooooooo!" Santa wailed seeing his last hope frozen where she stood, like a crystal ornament.

"Santa, you have been a naughty boy. You never told me that you had more flying reindeer?" the wizard sneered.

Now seeing his captor for the first time Santa begged, "You cannot do this! Olive is the only daughter of…"

"How dare you tell me what to do! I remind you sir, I can do whatever I want for I am the Blizzard Wizard!"

"No, my boy, you are John Blizzard of Oxford, England. The boy I brought his first toy sailing ship to at Christmas when he was just six years old," Santa reminded him gently.

"That was when I believed in you but now, you are just a pawn of humanity to fool the people into the illusion of hope!"

"I know that somewhere inside you is still the little boy who believes, just like your son Edward did all his life."

"My son! Bah! I left them when we set sail and I never saw him again nor my beloved wife!" Then he added, "Life abandoned me!"

"But they did not and nor did I. Every year in your absence I visited them on Christmas Eve to give them a little hope that you might return one day. And I always left a small gift to let Edward know he was never forgotten."

"How would you know I was not forgotten?"

"An extra plate was always placed at the head of dinner table, your favorite jacket hung behind your empty chair, and your picture hung above the fireplace," Santa recalled.

Chloe suddenly remembering that she still had the locket gripped in her talons made one great effort to fly and swooped down over the wizard, dropped the chain and locket on the wizards staff then swooped back up to another ledge.

"What is this?" he said gruffly, swatting at Chloe as she flew over him. Then he paused, "Wait a minute. I know this locket," he said taking it into his hand. For a brief moment his voice softened. "My darling gave this to me when we set sail from Portsmouth," he said with a quaver in his voice.

"They missed you every day and prayed to God for your safe return until the day they died," Santa said with compassion.

Visibly shaking the wizard opened the locket in his hands to reveal his most treasured pictures. "Is this a trick?" he snapped.

"We got it from the Red Eyed Raven! Whoot hoot!" Chloe said intently. "From the Red Eyed Raven, whoot hoot!" she repeated.

"The Raven?" he said as if remembering something long forgotten.

"Whoot hoot! Whoot hoot!"

For several moments no one moved or spoke then it seemed the evil cloud returned. "It changes nothing!" he screamed, snapping the locket shut, his eyes glowing with evil once more. "I am the Blizzard Wizard and I will show the world that there is no room for sentiment! No room for Santa Claus," he howled.

"But you can't," Santa pleaded.

The wizard raised his arms once more and cast another ice spell that shot out of his staff, sealing back the hole Olive had chipped out around Santa's face, then bouncing off and encasing Chloe in solid ice up on her ledge.

In complete despair Santa, Olive, and Chloe all thought the same thing at the same time: It's over.

CHAPTER TWENTY-FOUR
The Gatekeeper

The Blizzard Wizard turned briskly to leave the cave but stopped short in surprise. Another spirit stood in the entrance. With her white hair blowing wildly in the raging storm, and her arms outstretched to block the way, there stood a transformed elder dressed in traditional ceremonial dress of the Gwitch'in people. Olive knew her as Alice, the grandmother.

"Who are you?" demanded the wizard.

"I am the gatekeeper," she answered calmly.

"Gatekeeper? Gatekeeper of what?" he roared.

"The afterlife," she said as a glowing portal formed behind her.

"Out of my way, old woman! I have no time for this, this afterlife," he said twirling the locket and chain the same way as he had done many times before aboard the Red Eyed Raven.

"You shall not pass!" she said firmly. "You need to see your true path and it is not of this earth."

"The path I take is out there to show the world that it is morally corrupt and that humanity has no right to happiness, just as I have been denied for all this time!" He pointed his staff at the Gatekeeper and fired another lightning bolt. This time it bounced off her and careened into the night sky.

"You must be John Edward Blizzard. You have no place on this earth," she said, floating forward and forcing the wizard back into the cave.

"Why should I believe you? You are just an old woman," he said, visibly shaken at seeing another spirit who did not submit to his power.

"I am the Gatekeeper of the afterlife and I have walked this earth many more lifetimes than you could ever count. I say to you, once and for all, for you to find peace you must release your hold on this earth!"

"I must?"

"You must. Now open your locket and see the ones who love you dearly. Don't just look at them. See them."

The wizard opened the locket once more and gazed at the faces that looked lovingly back at him. For the first time in over a century a tear formed in the corner of his eye and trickled down his cheek and for a brief moment, long-forgotten comforting warmth filled his heart. "But, but these people are gone and no longer a part of my life."

"They may be gone and may indeed not be part of you in this life but they are still a part of you." She turned to one side. "Look, John Edward Blizzard, and see the life you should fulfill."

Standing in the entrance of the portal the wizard saw a group of familiar people appear, welcoming him with outstretched arms. "Who are these people?"

"Don't you recognize them, John? This is Edward, your son," she said pointing to an older gentleman in a Naval uniform.

"But…"

"Father, don't you know me?" the spirit said, transforming back into the boy his father remembered.

"My goodness! I do, I do. My Edward, my beloved Edward."

"I followed your footsteps into the Royal Navy, Father. I became a captain of my own ship by thirty-two and an admiral by fifty."

"What about me, my darling?" asked an older woman with neatly pinned grey hair and wearing an early Victorian, black mourning dress. "I am your wife, Julia, who never lost hope, not even once of your return."

"Julia? My Julia?" he asked as she too changed back into the form and wearing the same clothes she had when they had kissed farewell on the docks of Portsmouth.

"Yes, my darling," she answered tenderly.

"My love, I have missed you in the most eternal way." He reached for her hand. "Come to me."

"I cannot come to you, John. You are still standing in the land of the living and I have crossed over. If you wish to hold me once again, you must come to me," she said with shining eyes.

"But my love..." he said, completely confused. "I, I..."

"And these," she said, pointing to the others, "are all your grandsons and granddaughters, great-grandsons, and great-granddaughters. They wish to meet their famous and brave grandfather."

"This is what I have missed all this time?" he blubbered out loud, reaching for the hand of the youngest spirit.

"Yes, John," answered Alice. "It is not humanity that abandoned you, not Christmas, and not your family or any others. I am afraid that all belongs to you."

Ashamed, the wizard broke down completely, sobbing as he slumped to the floor. "What have I done?"

"Nothing you cannot make right," said Alice returning to her regular form and helping him up.

The Blizzard Wizard picked up his staff one last time, closed his eyes, and held it out in front of him. With the evil now faded from his face, the gentle spirit that had been held down inside him for so long bloomed like an opening flower. He had returned to being ancient mariner Captain John Edward Blizzard, the sea captain of the Red Eyed Raven. He softly spoke the incantation and cast his final spell.

A bolt of white light steamed from his staff and swirled around the room lighting it up like daylight and striking each of the captives in turn. Instantly, the ice mural encasing Santa, his sleigh, and the nine reindeer melted into pools on the cave floor allowing them to shake free the ice crystals and stiffness from being held motionless for so long. The blankets of ice encasing Olive and Chloe shattered like glass as they shook free from their frozen bonds.

Outside, the raging wind, thunder, and lightning all stopped their angry howls allowing the clouds to turn soft white and gently part to display a billion of sparkling stars shining in the clear night sky.

"I am so sorry, Father Christmas. I don't know how I could have been so wrong," John said looking around to the others, "and to all of you, as well. I don't know what came over me and I am so sorry for it all. I hope you can forgive me."

"Whoot hoot, I feel like a frozen dinner!" Chloe said, fluffing her feathers out.

"Ho, ho, ho," Santa chuckled in his familiar laugh. "I may have to bring you a piece of coal this Christmas, Captain!" he said causing the laughter of all.

"Thank you, Saint Nicholas," John said, hanging his head. "I promise to hold Christmas in my heart for however long I exist, in this world or the next. Is there anything I can do, Father Christmas?"

"You can join your family, ho, ho, ho," he said guiding him to the portal where the loving arms of his family reached out to accept him. Behind them, his generations of spirits, the ghosts of his crew also waited for him, including Second Lieutenant James Squire Pittman, the First Mate, and Mister Parker, the ship's helm.

Captain John Edward Blizzard took his wife's hand and with the first smile he had smiled in over a century, he stepped into the warm glow of the portal and walked into the light of the afterlife. Santa, Alice, Olive, and Chloe saw the Blizzard Wizard disappear for the last time when the portal gently closed as if it were never there at all.

"Thank you, Gatekeeper. I owe you so very much," Nicholas said to Alice after the spirits had left.

"Don't thank me, Christmas elf," Alice said kindly. "Your young reindeer here was the true hero of this adventure."

"Ho, ho, ho, I am sure she is!" he said looking at Olive. He nudged her up close to her papa, Prancer, and joyously greeted the other reindeer.

"Oh, Nicholas," Alice explained, "she risked her life many times to save you and her papa. If it wasn't for her distracting the wizard with the locket, I would not have been able to make him face his true path toward the afterlife."

"Well then, she will indeed receive a special reward when we return home to the North Pole," Santa said, giving Olive a loving cuddle around the neck.

"Grandpapa, I want no reward," Olive said as she snuggled happily under Santa's arm. "We all just wanted to get our Grandpapa and our family home! After all, what would Christmas be without Santa and his reindeer and all of us home for Christmas?"

"Ho, ho, ho, of course you did, little one. Thank-you from the bottom of my heart for being so brave."

"But I couldn't have done it without my friend, Chloe," Olive said.

"And who is Chloe?" Santa asked.

"Chloe the Snowy Owl," she said, beckoning Chloe down from her perch.

When the bird swooped down onto her usual perch atop Olive's antlers, Santa's laugh boomed throughout the cave. "Ho, ho, ho, how do you do Chloe?" he said shaking her good wing.

"Whoot hoot, better the second time than the first!"

"Second time?" Santa asked.

"I'll explain later, Grandpapa. It's a long story, but Chloe has stuck by me all the way and she is my friend."

"That is good enough for me. Thank-you, Chloe, for all your help."

"No problem, whoot hoot."

Alice stepped forward. "I must take my leave, Nicholas," she said. "I must return to my people and get back to the real world." She turned to Olive and Chloe. "You see, Olive, it's not only you that must keep secrets," she said with a wink.

"Secrets are things we give others to keep for us, whoot hoot!"

"So true, Chloe," the old lady answered. "Make sure you come and visit me, Olive."

"I will, I will, Grandmother, but what about Chloe?"

"I would like to ask Chloe if she wants to come with me until her wing gets better."

"Wow, Chloe, that is a nice offer," Olive said, "but I will miss you terribly."

"Ho, ho, ho," Santa chuckled, "you are more than welcome to stay at the North Pole for as long as you like."

"What do you think, Chloe?" Alice said.

"I am so thankful I have found so many friends on my adventure, especially Olive. Whoot hoot! Owls never have many friends," Chloe cooed. "But I don't believe the North Pole is where a Snowy owl should spend the rest of her days. Next year I'm going to head east instead of North, whoot hoot. Hopefully I won't run into a sack of toys! Whoot hoot."

"Is that what you did?" Santa questioned. "Oh my, I didn't see you, my feathered friend. I would have certainly stopped had I known. Please come back with us. Carol and I would love to have you stay until you get better."

"Thank-you, Santa, but I think I will go with Grandmother, whoot hoot."

"Really?" Olive said sadly. "I was hoping you would stay with us."

"My wing is feeling stronger every day and I'm already half way home. But as you must go home so must I, whoot hoot."

"We both know Grandmother can cure you better than I can," Olive said, tears gathering on her lashes. "But I really hate to see you go."

"As soon as you are ready, Chloe, we must go," Alice told her.

Chloe fluttered as best she could down onto the Gwitch'in elder's shoulder. "Good-bye Olive," she said with tears in her round eyes.

"Good-bye, Chloe. I will be sure to visit you." Olive gave Alice a nuzzle in thanks. "I will visit you too, Grandmother, when the coast is clear and Akliak is busy elsewhere."

With final hugs, Alice and Chloe quietly disappeared out into the winter.

"Distance never separates good friends, Olive," Santa said, "and I know you will see her again. We will make sure of that, ho, ho, ho! Now, I cannot wait to hear all about your adventure." Santa climbed back into his sleigh and grabbed the reins.

Olive glanced at the waiting team then back at the sleigh. "Where should I go, Grandpapa?"

"You, my dear, will be at the front with Rudolph to take us home," Santa said. The other reindeer broke into smiles, especially her proud father, Prancer.

"Really, Grandpapa? Am I going to be your tenth reindeer from now on?"

"Ho, ho, ho. We'll see about that, young lady, but for our journey home you certainly are, ho, ho, ho!"

"Yippee!" Olive squealed and dashed to the front of the team.

As they swooshed out the cave and into the air with Olive in the lead, she turned to Rudolf. "Which way do we go?

"That-a-way," the entire team all shouted together.

With the rest of the reindeer, Olive then headed north with Santa chuckling in the back. "Ho, ho, ho!"

CHAPTER TWENTY-FIVE
The Homecoming

At the North Pole the excitement couldn't be contained after hearing that Santa and all of the reindeer were safe and sound and on their way home, including Olive! Several stations on Santa's Hot Line had relayed the message. The elves and Mrs. Claus all clasped hands and merrily danced around the kitchen until they fell down exhausted and giddy with laughter.

"Oh, my goodness!" Mrs. Claus exclaimed, looking at the clock. "Santa and the reindeer will be home soon and we must be ready! All of you, off you go now and let's get busy," she said clapping her hands.

The elves dashed away to make sure the stables were in tiptop order with fresh hay, straw, blankets, and reindeer treats in each of the stalls. They included a something little extra for Olive.

Alabaster stacked all the incoming mail in order. He placed the new treats to one side so that everything was ready for Santa to nibble on when Mrs. Claus wasn't looking. The workshop elves swept the floor, turned off all the machines and conveyer belts, and made sure the gifts were wrapped and loaded on the newly painted spare sleigh ready for delivery for those children who celebrated

Christmas on January sixth. Finally, when all was spic and span, Sparkles turned on all the outside Christmas lights.

Mrs. Claus lit the lights on the Christmas tree. Christmas songs wafted softly from the record player, and she stoked the fire to make sure the living room was warm and cozy once again. She had always believed that there was something magical about a room filled with hope and expectation—and smelled like candy canes and cinnamon. Once satisfied that the living room looked just right, she hurriedly set the table with Pukki and Sparkles to help her, then went off to the kitchen to start preparing a wonderful Christmas dinner. There was so much to do in such a short time but she was determined they would have their Christmas with all its trimmings, even if a few days late.

When all was ready, a line of faces gazed from every frosted window. As in every year, the one who saw Rudolph's nose first received an extra candy cane as an award from Mrs. Claus, even though she often saw the glow before any of the elves had.

"There it is!" Sparky shouted, wildly hopping up and down.

"Are you sure, Sparky? I can't see anything," said Mrs. Claus peering into the darkness.

"I'm sure it was, Grandmama," he said looking again.

"I think you are fooling me to get the extra candy cane," teased Mrs. Claus.

"I see it too!" hollered Sprinkles from the upper window.

"We too, we too," Pere Noel and Papai Noel both squealed.

Mrs. Claus looked again and sure enough, the red glow from Rudolph's nose was growing brighter by the second.

"Yes, yes! It's Grandpapa!" said little Pukki.

"All right," Mrs. Claus surrendered. "You shall all get a candy cane!" Her announcement met with boisterous squeals. "Okay, okay, settle down. Let's get ready for Santa. Babbo and Ripplo, please go and open the launch bay doors. Bingo, please have Santa's slippers ready at the door. Sprinkles, get his sweater, and I'll pour the hot chocolate. I think they all deserve a treat, don't you think?" She was met with another chorus of cheers.

For Olive, the ride home seemed too short. Being in the lead for Santa's team for the very first time was thrilling, but when she saw the doors open, she was excited to be home.

"Okay Olive, start slowing down so we can make a gentle landing," Rudolph coached.

"That's it. Nice and easy," shouted Santa from the rear.

They glided in and gently touched down inside the landing bay. "Ho, ho ho! How wonderful to see you all," Santa boomed as Babbo and Ripplo closed the doors behind the sleigh.

"Are you all right, Nicholas?" Mrs. Claus cried as she ran to greet him.

"Why yes, my dear, but I must say it certainly was an adventure."

"I am so happy that you are all home, safe and sound," Mrs. Claus sighed.

"With all that we've been through, we certainly do have a lot to be thankful for. Olive told me all about her dangerous mission on our way home. She was very brave and did a spectacular job." He gave Olive a loving pat on the neck.

"You will have to tell us all about it after a nice Christmas dinner, Olive," said Mrs. Claus.

"And the present openings!" shouted the elves.

The other reindeer also wanted to hear all about Olive's adventure. She would be a legend amongst the reindeer for all time for her bravery in saving Santa.

"We were all so worried," Alabaster said.

"Thank-you to all of you," Santa said, standing up. "To my faithful team, to our brave Olive, and to all of you. I could sense your prayers; they helped me keep the faith that we would soon be rescued." He then turned to his wife, Carol. "And you, my sweet, I felt you beside me all the way." He hugged and kissed her as the elves cheered.

"Oh, Nicholas, not in front of the children," she said, blushing pink.

"We must also thank Olive's friends who helped her on her journey," he recalled as they walked toward the house. "Alabaster, write these names on our Nice List and make sure they each get an extra special gift."

"Yes, Grandpapa, who shall I put down?" he said pulling a paper and pen from his chest pocket.

"Let me see, Chloe, the Snowy Owl, for sure. She was struck by the sleigh and it injured her wing."

"Oh, Grandpapa, give her something very special," Olive begged as she skipped along beside him.

"Then there's Sly and his family Stone, an arctic fox who saved Olive from a sinking ship."

"Sinking ship?" Alabaster wondered about that story but simply replied, "Yes, Grandpapa."

"Bruce the Christmoose, for protecting Olive and Chloe from White Storm and his Howling Dozen."

"Oh, I know Bruce. He's a Santa's Helper in training. He called us on the Hot Line to let us know about Olive."

"I think he deserves to be an Official Santa's Helper from now on, don't you? Ho, ho, ho!"

"Of course, Grandpapa."

"A boy in Fort Yukon by the name of Akliak saved Olive from White Storm and his Howling Dozen, too."

"White Storm again?"

"Yes, Alabaster. There was even a third time, when he chased her on the ice," Santa mused.

"Coal?"

"Yes, a piece of coal for each of those wolves. For the next several years, I think! Ho, ho, ho!"

"Is that it, Grandpapa?"

"Oh, goodness no. We cannot forget about Alice, Akliak's grandmother. She is the Gatekeeper to the Afterlife and an Elder of the Gwitch'in people. She helped Olive in so many ways and led the Blizzard Wizard into the afterlife.

"Blizzard Wizard, Grandpapa?"

"I'll tell you all about him after dinner, but now let's get something to eat before I waste away to nothing, ho, ho, ho!" he chortled loudly, rubbing chubby tummy.

"Yes, Grandpapa. I can smell the turkey roasting all the way out here," Alabaster said as they walked into the living room to find all the elves gathered, waiting for Christmas to start.

With hot chocolate in hand, Santa sat down in his overstuffed chair by the fire and looked at all the shining, happy faces before him. And he thanked God they were all home, safe and sound.

After the carols were sung, the gifts opened, and the dinner and desserts gratefully received, Santa relayed to the eager ears and wide-eyed faces the story Olive had told him on their way home from Denali.

Once all was told and the yawns began, they sleepily went off to bed. When the house grew quiet and the lights turned out, the North Pole resounded in the Santa's familiar announcement:

"Ho, Ho, Ho! Merry Christmas to all and to all a good night!"

And in the warm stable Olive lay curled up in her bed of soft, fresh straw, fast asleep.

The Witch of Weasel Warren is a delightfully fun and spooky story is based in the fantasy town of Weasel Warren. An evil witch and warlock scheming to return Halloween into something more evil set out to have her weasel minions steal all the pumpkins from a local farmers pumpkin patch as part of her dastardly plan.

Duke Skysquawker, a crow from the Northwoods catches them in the act and reports it to his farm animal friends. Sneezer, the Bloodhound, Quacks, the pig, a raccoon named Stranger and Pronto, his sidekick field mouse, the Sugarplum Fairy, and Gerome the Gnome set out to thwart the evil plan.

BOOKS BY BRUCE KILBY AND KEN JOHNSON

In the medieval town of Bicuspid on the Root Canal, the secrets of why the tooth fairy comes for children's teeth had been long forgotten until an adventurous young boy named Garth wanted to become friends with a dragon named Fangor.

His innocence gets him into a lot of trouble, as little did he know that in the process, he would create the ancient dragon wars and upset the long friendships between fairies, dragons and humans. With many bumps along the road, Garth becomes the hero with the help from his friends turning back the evil Pyorrhoea Pete the Pirate, his henchwoman Ginger Vitis and the hoard of bat-like Drooling Gummies.

The book has many references to teeth and dental hygiene as well as being exciting for children to read. The book also comes with a Tooth Fairy's Tooth (a tooth or coin safekeeping container) making it easier for the tooth fairy to find in the middle of the night.

This exciting adventure sequel continues in the modern day city of Bicuspid from the escapades of 800 years ago by the magician Garth, described in *The Legend of the Tooth Fairy* by a magical teddy bear by the name of Taddy Boy.

Fangor, the last remaining dragon, has sensed dragon eggs have been unearthed in a place called Gumgolia and, driven by strong prehistoric survival instincts, he wishes to bring them back to life. Holly, the unsuspecting young descendant of Garth, is summoned by the fairies to help them in a magical and dangerous journey through Brusha, Tonsilvania, and the Land of Plaque.

Once again the evil bats called the Drooling Gummies, under their Emperor, Ruthless Toothless Brutus, and his queen, Hali Tosis, have returned to spread their Nightmare Dust, capture fairies and, at all costs, to seize the last dragon.

With the help from her friends Taddy Boy, T-Pick the chameleon, Hip Hop the Praying Mantis, and several others along the way, Holly becomes a Dragon Rider and Magician's Apprentice in her quest to save the dragons and all the Fairylands.

ABOUT THE ARTISTS

Christine Lee was born in Vancouver and raised in Surrey, B.C. and is currently studying at Emily Carr University where she hopes to pursue animation or concept art. She likes to listen to music and write short stories. She specializes in traditional work, mainly with watercolours and pens.

Wendy Dewar Hughes is an artist, editor, book designer, and is the author of over twenty books. Her art and designs appear on books, gifts, travel products, clothing, and home goods. She lives in a village in British Columbia. Her work can be found at www.wendydewarhughes.com, and www.summerbaypress.com.